Dear Reader,

Love at first sight can be a dream come true, but sometimes second chances can be even sweeter. This month, four breathtaking new romances from Bouquet prove it!

Veteran author Colleen Faulkner starts us off with the first in the new Bachelors, Inc. miniseries, **Marrying Owen,** the story of an estranged couple forced into close quarters by a sudden storm—and ready to give love another try. Next up is the final installment in Vivian Leiber's the Men of Sugar Mountain trilogy, **Three Wishes.** When a man from her past returns to her small town, one woman wonders if he's now the key to the future she's always hoped for.

Sometimes romance blooms in the most unexpected places. That's what happens when the heroine of Wendy Morgan's **Ask Me Again** finds herself in a wedding party with the most boring guy she knew in college—and discovers he's become a fascinating and sexy man. Finally, Susan Hardy proves that every cloud really does have a **Silver Lining** when an accident that threatens everything one woman has leads her into the arms of a man who becomes the one thing she really wants.

Laughter, tears, desire, and most of all, love—Bouquet delivers them all. Why not give one a chance today?

Kate Duffy
Editorial Director

KISSING OWEN

Abby stretched out on her side so that she lay parallel to Owen with the board between them. How many games of Scrabble had they played like this over the years? She tried to concentrate on her available letters and beating him rather than on his blue eyes following her every move. He seemed to be breathing in time with her, making her entirely too aware of his body and her own. She wrote *doomed*. Was she?

Her hand was barely back from the board when he dropped his tiles into place. *You.*

He had written *Kiss you.*

She looked up at him, her gaze meeting his. His mouth was slightly upturned in a smile that told her he was unsure of himself.

"How did you manage that?" she asked softly, mesmerized by his eyes, by his mouth and the overwhelming need she felt to kiss him. "Are you cheating?" she accused.

He shook his head, refusing to look away.

"You asking?" she breathed.

"I think so." His words came out in a whisper.

Abby didn't say yes, but she didn't say no. She felt frozen in time as he inched across the carpet toward her.

Owen's lips brushed hers and her eyes closed of their own accord. She could feel herself melting into the carpet. It had been so long since he had kissed her like that. A kiss she felt to the tips of her toes. And he was such a good kisser. . . .

BACHELORS INC.:
MARRYING OWEN

Colleen Faulkner

Zebra Books
Kensington Publishing Corp.

http://www.zebrabooks.com

ZEBRA BOOKS are published by

Kensington Publishing Corp.
850 Third Avenue
New York, NY 10022

First Printing: August, 2000
10 9 8 7 6 5 4 3 2 1

Printed in the United States of America

Prologue

August, 1974

Ten-year-old Owen Thomas beat his fist on the door of the garden shed behind Ben Gordon's house. "Let me in!" he shouted. Pressing his back to the door, he scanned the backyard for signs of infiltrators. "Hurry up!"

Abby Maconnal had tried to talk to him as he passed the post office on his bike, but he'd pedaled right by her as if she didn't exist. He was sure she hadn't followed him. Abby was always trying to talk to him because it was his bad luck to have moved right next door to her only three weeks ago.

Owen spotted a movement that turned out to be a sprinkler spraying a flower bed. He saw an abandoned lawn chair and his bike where he'd left it in the middle of the lawn, but no Abby. He shifted the paper bag he carried to his other hand and pounded. "Open up!"

"Password?" Zack hissed from the other side of the door.

Zack and Ben were his two best friends in the little

town of Land's End, perched on the eastern edge of the Chesapeake Bay. His best friends in the whole world.

"Beans and franks," Owen said.

The two boys inside the shed sniggered. "Say it right, Owen, or you don't get in," Ben warned.

Owen scratched at a mosquito bite on his elbow. "This is stupid."

"You know the rules. You have to say it if you want to get in . . ."

He could hear the two boys laughing. Owen wanted to get in. Being new in town, he wanted desperately to belong to the new club they were forming. He wanted buddies before he had to go to his new school next month and start fifth grade; he just hated saying this stupid password.

"Say it," Zack coaxed. "Come on, Owen; then we'll let you in."

Owen rolled his eyes. He could smell the fresh-cut lawn; a dog was barking next door. Probably at him. He exhaled. "Beans and farts," he whispered.

"Gotta say it *lou . . . der*," Ben teased.

"Beans and farts!" Owen shouted.

Thankfully, the door swung open.

Owen ducked inside, red-faced, embarrassed and excited all at the same time. His mom and dad didn't let him say *fart,* but what they didn't know wouldn't hurt them, would it?

"What did you bring?" Zack slammed the door and locked it from the inside.

The boys had bought a hook-and-eye at Smitty's Hardware store just yesterday and installed it themselves, getting ready for their new club. The hook was a little lower than the eye so that they had to really tug to get the door closed and locked, but it worked and the boys were proud of their handiwork.

Owen plopped down on the shed floor beside a lawn mower and opened the crumpled paper bag. "Two orange crushes, some root beer barrels and a moon pie."

Zack flopped on the plywood floor beside him, Ben across from them so that they formed a circle. Sunlight poured in through the small, open window in the back. The shed was hot and smelled of old grass and rose fertilizer, but no one cared. They were in their private domain now.

"Only two sodas and one moon pie?" Ben asked, pushing his Baltimore Orioles ball cap around so that the brim faced backward. "But there are three of us."

Owen brushed his sandy blond hair off his forehead. His mom said it was shaggy and needed cutting, but Owen liked it. Secretly, he thought it made him look like his favorite TV character—Starsky on "Starsky and Hutch."

"We'll just share," Owen defended. "I don't really like moon pies anyway." He pushed the food to the center of the circle the boys formed with their open legs. "What did you guys bring?"

"Red licorice," Ben said, whipping it out of the back pocket of his cut-off jean shorts.

"Sunflower seeds." Zack waved a plastic baggie. His mom and dad were the local hippies; his mom said every town had them. The Taylors bought everything in bulk.

"Sunflower seeds?" Owen laughed, turning to Zack. He was wearing a tie-died T-shirt and a headband around his head. His hair was even longer than Owen's. "Who eats sunflower seeds?"

"I do and you would if you had any sense." Zack popped one into his mouth and cracked the shell between his teeth. "You know how many vitamins are in sunflower seeds? You need your protein, man. How else you going to get rid of those scrawny city-boy shoulders?" He gave Owen a push, spitting the empty shell onto the floor.

Owen pushed him back. Nothing rough, just guy stuff. It made Owen feel good to have someone to push. He hadn't wanted to move from Wilmington to Land's End. He hadn't wanted to make new friends, but it wasn't like his parents had given him a choice. He knew he was lucky to have found Zack and Ben.

"Hey! Come on," Ben said, ever the diplomat. "Are we going to do this or not?"

The three ten-year-olds met each other's gazes and nodded.

"We're gonna do it," Zack said with conviction.

"We're gonna do it," Owen repeated with equal fervor.

"OK, so how do we do it? Blood?" Ben asked.

"Blood?" Zack wrinkled his nose. "Like cutting our wrists and letting our blood run together?"

Owen laughed. "Not your wrist, butt-head. You'd die. On TV they just prick fingers."

All three boys looked at each other again. They all wanted to make the pact, but no one seemed to be enthusiastic about the blood idea. Owen knew he had to think quick before they gave up on the idea and decided to ride bikes instead.

"OK, OK," Owen said holding up his hands. "That's boring. Been done. I got a better idea."

"What?"

"Give me the moon pie."

Ben pushed the cellophane-wrapped chocolate-and-marshmallow cake across the floor.

"And one of the cans of soda."

Zack passed the soda.

Owen pulled a bandana from his back pocket, the one he wore to keep his hair back when they were jumping ditches with their bikes, and laid it out on the floor between his legs. He then ripped open the moon pie and laid it on the red bandana. Both boys watched in anticipation, making him feel important. He pulled the tab on the can of soda and put the drink beside the moon pie.

"We sure about this?" Owen asked, trying to make his voice deep so he would sound official. "Because men don't enter pacts like this easily. It's a big responsibility."

"I'm ready," Ben said, making a fist and jerking his arm back in a show of strength.

Zack drew up his legs and folded them Indian style as if he were meditating. "I'm ready," he said serenely, resting his forearms on his knees.

"Then let's get started." Owen lowered his head. "We three present do hereby form the GAG Club. By sharing this bread and this wine—"

"It's a moon pie and soda," Ben whispered.

Zack elbowed him.

"We do hereby swear our oath," Owen continued. "We swear by each other not to play with girls, talk to them in school unless we have to, and most important, we swear not to dance with any of them at any fifth grade dances."

Owen picked up the moon pie, took a bite, and passed it to Zack. Then he lifted the can of orange crush to his lips and took a sip of the warm soda. The two tastes didn't go together, but he didn't care. It was symbolic. This would make the three boys friends forever, wouldn't it?

The boys solemnly passed the pie and soda around in a circle until it came back to Owen. He returned the food to the bandana.

"Amen," he whispered.

"Amen," the other two repeated.

Owen glanced up at his new friends. He felt good inside, like maybe Land's End might be an OK town after all. "It's final then, we are the three official members of the GAG Club."

"Girls Are Gross," Zack said with a grin.

A bang on the door of the shed startled all three of them.

"Who is it?" Ben shouted.

All three scrambled to their feet. It couldn't be Ben's mom or dad. They were at work. And his older sister, who kept an eye on him, was on the phone. She was always on the phone.

"It's Abby," came a girl's voice. "Is Owen in there?"

Zack and Ben turned to Owen as if he had just betrayed them to the enemy.

Owen made a face. "I didn't tell her where we were," he whispered. "She's such a pain."

Abby banged on the door again. "Owen, I know you're in there. I saw your bike. I'm going to the library. You want to go?" She paused. "It's got to be a lot cooler at the library than in that dumb shed."

Owen stared at the door. He didn't know what to do. He was trapped. Maybe his friends would just kill him now and put him out of his misery. Save what little honor he had left. Of course, the only thing they would be able to kill him with in this shed would be a rusty pair of garden shears and he wasn't sure he wanted to die that badly.

"Get rid of her," Ben hissed.

"Get rid of her," Zack echoed.

"How?"

Ben pushed him toward the door. "That's your problem."

Before Owen could protest, Ben yanked open the door and Zack pushed him out. The shed door slammed shut before he could turn back. Suddenly he was face-to-face with pretty Abby Maconnal.

She grinned, planting her hands on her hips. She wore her blondish brown hair over her shoulders with a little braid on each side. She had on jean shorts and a sleeveless shirt. Her eyes were bluer than anything Owen had ever seen.

"I . . . I'm not going to the library with you," he stammered. "Stop following me."

She shrugged. "Fine. Suit yourself. I just thought you might want to get a book. You know we're coming to dinner tonight to your house. My parents and me. They'll send us off after dinner to *play*. I just thought that if we had books we wouldn't have to actually say anything to each other." She flipped one hand. "But, whatever."

Owen stared at his black canvas sneakers. He didn't know what to say. It was a good plan, but his friends were listening. And he needed to get rid of her before their teasing became merciless. He started to walk toward his bike to lead her away from the shed so Zack and Ben couldn't hear what they were saying.

"Maybe later," he said quietly.

Her bike was beside his in the grass. "OK. Whatever."

Again, she shrugged a suntanned shoulder. He noticed there were freckles there, like little brown dots. He couldn't stop looking at them.

"I . . . I'm supposed to get a haircut later. Maybe after that," he mumbled.

She looked up at him with those blue eyes. "Get your hair cut! Don't tell me your mom's going to make you get your hair cut." She uprighted her bike and climbed onto the purple banana seat. "It's so cool. It makes you look just like Starsky."

Owen was still grinning when ten-year-old Abby Maconnal rode her bike around the house and disappeared from his sight.

One

"Hey, guys. Sorry I'm late." Owen slid onto the vinyl booth bench at the Pizza Palace in the little town of Land's End.

"Dude," Zack said from behind his laminated menu.

"No problem. We just got here ourselves." Ben tossed him a menu across the table. "Ordered a pitcher."

"Great." Owen scanned the menu, but he was too excited to care what he ordered. "Pizza's fine," he said, dropping the menu to the Formica table. "Whatever toppings."

"Careful there, or Flower Power here will order sunflower seed and tofu pizza for us," Ben warned with a grin.

"That or ginseng and arugula."

Owen and Ben laughed.

This was what was great about being together again. They could laugh and make foolish, juvenile jokes and not worry about what anyone thought about them. It was the perfect way to deal with life's blows.

"Very funny. The two of you are a barrel of laughs." Zack added his menu to the pile. "Actually, I was thinking more on the lines of green peppers, black olives, and mushrooms, but if tofu is what you want—"

"Veggies work for me." Owen clapped his hands. "So, are we set, gentlemen?"

"Got our business license at the chamber today and picked up the incorporation papers at the attorney's," Ben said. "It's all worked up; all we have to do is sign and give him a name for the company."

"A name?" Owen sat back. "We've been so busy working on the details that I hadn't thought about a name. Have you?" He looked up at the two men who had been his closest friends for over twenty years. The two friends who hadn't abandoned him, not since the summer between fourth and fifth grade when he'd arrived in town. They'd been there for him through college and grad school, through job changes, his wedding and the divorce that still left him feeling hollow inside. He loved them like brothers.

Owen had returned to Land's End last month to live and to run a business they had dreamed up a year ago. After living life in the fast lane, trying their luck at love, big business and big cities, they had all come to the conclusion that they belonged in Land's End together. On paper, they had created a business of restoring old homes to their past glory. Owen, an architect, would design additions and improvements to structures without altering their original design. Ben would serve as the general contractor, hiring whatever workmen were needed. Zack, the man of talented hands, would use his extraordinary cabinetmaking skills to recreate fireplace mantels, hand-carved dentil molding and kitchen cupboards. They already had two customers and had only to finish the paperwork.

"A name, a name," Zack said thoughtfully. "Land's End Restorations doesn't work? I thought that was what we agreed on. Simple, and to the point."

"That's the name of the company," Ben pointed out. "But our corporation needs a different name. That way, if we create new companies in the future—"

"They'll still fall under the corporate name," Owen said.

"Exactly."

A waitress brought them a pitcher of light beer and three mugs. Ben poured.

"A name that represents the three of us," Owen thought aloud and grinned. "How about the GAG Club?"

Zack and Ben laughed.

"Jeez, I haven't thought of that in years," Zack said.

"Girls Are Gross . . ." Ben pushed a mug of beer to Owen.

"We'd probably have been better off if we'd stuck to our vows, eh?" Owen said, trying not to sound too dismal.

He thought of Abby—pretty, freckled Abby Maconnal. The girl next door. He hadn't danced with her in the fifth grade, but by the time they reached junior high they were "going together," and dated on and off through high school. They'd gone to college at the University of Delaware and then she'd followed him to NYU where he got a master's degree and she worked to put him through school and put cheeseburgers on the table. They married and everyone thought they would live happily ever after. They had been together so long. Meant for each other. Then one day a year ago Owen woke up in their apartment in Boston and Abby was gone . . .

Owen lifted his mug.

"Hey wait," Ben said. "You can't drink until we come up with a name."

Owen lowered his mug, trying to switch gears, trying to push Abby out of his mind as he'd been trying to do since the morning she left him. Hell, he didn't even really know why she left. "A name, a name. And GAG Club won't work?"

Ben lifted a dark eyebrow. He was considered the best-looking one of the three of them. Women went crazy over him. He'd dated fashion models, rich older women, and even a pop star in California. But sooner or later they'd all left him or he'd left them. Ben had never been married and swore he never would be.

"No, the GAG Club will not work," Zack said, tugging on his ponytail. After Zack's divorce, he had left his fancy job and ritzy house in Annapolis and come home to raise his daughter Savannah in the house he'd grown up in. It was Zack who had come up with the idea of starting a company together. It was Zack who had lured Owen and Ben back to Land's End with the promise of peace and comfortable living. Maybe even happiness. It was what they all seemed to crave, though none of them could actually come out and say it.

"No, GAG Club won't work."

"OK," Owen conceded. But it should be something like that. Something fun."

Owen wracked his brain. The three of them had formed the GAG Club in '76 on the basis of friendship without the need of women. He glanced up. "I've got it."

"Well? Out with it. The beer is getting warm."

He leaned back on the bench. "Bachelors, Incorporated."

Zack scratched his short red beard. "Bachelors, Incorporated?"

"Sure. Bachelors, Inc. A grown-up version of the GAG Club."

"I think you may be on to something, brother," Zack said with a grin.

Ben nodded. "Bachelors, Inc. I like it. Rolls off the tongue." He gestured with a flourish.

"See, we can make a decision." Owen reached for his mug again. "If we're all in agreement, Bachelors, Inc. it is."

"Bachelors, Inc.," the three thirty-something men said, raising their beer mugs. Glass clinked as they toasted.

Owen took a swallow of the cold beer. It felt so good to be home. Home with Zack and Ben and all the things that were so familiar to him. The Pizza Palace, Smitty's Hardware, the library where he had spent so many happy hours. It even felt good to be in Abby's parents' house, despite some of the memories that now left an ache inside him. He had bought the place from her in the divorce settlement and moved in a month ago. Zack and Ben had thought it might be weird for him to live in his ex-wife's parents' house, but it wasn't. He was right next door to his own aging parents and could keep an eye on them as they grew older and needed him more. And somehow, though he wouldn't admit it to the guys, being in Abby's old house was comforting. It made him feel closer to her, not so alone in the world.

Ben gripped his mug. "So, while we're toasting to the reformation of the GAG Club, now known as Bachelors, Inc., what say we make a vow."

Owen chuckled. Zack just stared at Ben as if he were nuts.

"A vow?"

"Once upon a time we all promised each other we would stay away from girls," Ben said. "And you know, we'd all have been better off if we'd just taken our own advice."

"I know I would have been," Zack muttered, not knowing if Ben was serious or not.

"Women have gotten me nothing but trouble and heartache," Ben said.

"Wouldn't surprise me if you picked up something else, too." Zack winked at Owen.

Owen laughed.

"Hey, I'm serious here!" Ben protested. "I think we should reaffirm our vow to lay off women."

"We've got each other, our new business." Owen stared into his beer mug, thinking about what a mess he'd made of his marriage. He didn't really blame Abby, but women were so difficult to understand, even the ones you thought you knew. "What do we need women for?"

"My thought exactly," Ben said. "It sounds dumb, but

with the new business starting up the last thing any of us needs is that kind of distraction. After all, let's face it, we all have made poor choices in the past."

"So, no dating?" Zack asked.

Owen was fascinated by the idea. It sounded good to him. Safe. He had been so hurt after Abby had taken off.

Ben nodded. "No dating."

"I can see us handling it, but you?" Zack lifted an eyebrow.

"Hey, I've had it with women."

"And we'll be here for each other if anyone begins to slide off the slippery slope." Owen lifted his mug again. "Works for me. I've had my fill of women for one lifetime."

"You know I have," Zack agreed.

Again, Ben lifted his mug in toast. "So, it's no women for the bachelors three."

"No women," Zack and Owen echoed.

Owen took a drink of the beer and whispered under his breath. "Amen."

A few minutes later the pizza arrived and the men began to discuss their first two jobs. Owen had a job cut out for him with one of them. The owners of a colonial Georgian brick wanted to add a three-car garage without taking away from the ambience of the original white-washed structure. It was going to be a bear, but he already had some ideas. He figured he could put in five or six hours a day at his drafting table and still have time to sail his new sailboat. The winds were perfect on the Chesapeake Bay in August.

They were just finishing up the pizza when Zack's

daughter Savannah came into the Pizza Palace, leading Ben's father, Max. Apparently the two had been feeding ducks down on the shore.

"You two want a piece of pizza?" Owen slid over and made room for Savannah beside him.

Max pulled up a chair at the end of the booth. "Ate earlier," Max said.

"And then we had ice cream." Savannah grinned.

Knowing few children, Owen was fascinated by Savannah and amazed that Zack could be such a damned good single father. None of his and Abby's friends had had children; they were all career-oriented couples. He and Abby had once talked of having children—

"Not strawberry, I hope," said Zack.

Ten-year-old Savannah rolled her eyes. "Daddy thinks I'm allergic to strawberries."

"You are. They give you a rash." Zack mugged at his daughter. "We're about done here so we can go home."

"We don't have to." Savannah wiggled down the bench closer to Owen. "I like it here with Uncle Owen and Uncle Ben. Uncle Owen always gives me his crusts."

Owen plucked one off his paper plate and handed it to the little girl.

"So, what have you boys been up to? Get your business straightened out?" Max asked. He was a widower and baby-sat for Zack when he needed a sitter. Max said Savannah gave him a way to be useful and he adored the little girl as if she were his own granddaughter.

"Business taken care of, Pop." Ben looked to the other two men. "We agreed on Bachelors, Incorporated for the incorporation name."

Max lifted a bushy gray eyebrow. "Bachelors, Inc.? Hell of a name, son."

"But very appropriate," Owen explained. "We've decided to keep that status."

"Permanent bachelors?"

"You bet." Owen gestured. "You're welcome to be an honorary member. All you have to do is swear off women forever."

Max climbed out of his chair, chuckling. "You boys tickle me. Bachelors for life! You just haven't met the right women, that's what I say."

"So, you're not interested, eh, Pop?"

"Hell, no! I was married to your mother for almost forty years." Max waggled a finger at Ben. "Happiest years of my life. I aim to find me another wife. Not to replace your mother, mind you, but just to replace that empty spot in here." He tapped his chest over his heart.

"Well, if you change your mind, let us know," Owen offered. "There's always room for you, Max."

"Not only am I not interested in swearing off women for life, I'm not even interested in it for the day. So, if you men are done with me, I've got to get home and get showered. I've got a date at the senior center tonight."

Zack laughed. "Thanks for looking after Savannah while we settled our business. I appreciate it."

"No problem." Max waved. "Behave yourselves, boys. Don't do anything I wouldn't." Seventy-seven-year-old Max gave a wink and sauntered off.

* * *

Colleen Faulkner

When Owen got home, the answering machine on the table in the front hallway was blinking. Messages. He hit the play button as he riffled through his mail.

"Owen dear, it's Mother. Just checking to see if you wanted to join us for dinner. You must have found something to do. Maybe a date." She sounded hopeful. "Call me later. Bye." She made a kissing sound and the machine beeped, signaling the end of one message and the beginning of another.

The next message was a solicitation for a credit card— low initial interest percentage and frequent flyer miles. The cable company wanted to know if he wanted the exclusive movie package, including the "Men's After Hours" channel. He flipped through his junk mail as the machine came to the last message.

"Owen—"

He glanced up, stunned. It was Abby. He hadn't heard from her in over six months. He automatically leaned toward the machine—as if that could possibly bring him closer to her.

"I . . . I'm passing through Land's End this weekend. I thought I would stop by. There are some things stored in the attic I'd like to pick up."

She paused.

Owen held his breath.

"If that's a problem, call me. You know the number. Otherwise . . . I guess I'll see you Saturday."

Beep.

Owen replayed the message three times. He hoped hearing the sound of her voice over and over again would numb him. Remind him of how much she had hurt him when she walked out of his life for no tangible reason. He hoped that hearing her soft hesitant voice again and again would make him want to call her and tell her this weekend didn't suit.

All it did was make him want to see her more.

Two

Abby signaled and pulled her car over to the side of the road, coming to a stop just in front of the sign welcoming visitors to Land's End. Land's End, "Eden on the Chesapeake" it advertised, with pictures of waves and seashells. Below the billboard metal medallions were attached, noting that there was a Kiwanis Club, Kid's League Baseball, and Lions Club in town. A tumble of weeds blew by, followed by a discarded paper cup. The wind was picking up; a storm was blowing in.

Abby gripped the wheel tightly as she stared at the sign and considered turning around and heading south again. If traffic wasn't too bad she could be back on Interstate 95 in an hour. She could be headed south to Myrtle Beach where she'd rented a friend's empty beach house for a year. That's how long she was giving herself to write the book. One year. That was how long she figured her money would hold out.

Abby stared at the Land's End sign again, watching how the Kiwanis sign wobbled in the wind. She could smell rain in the air through the window, which was open a crack.

She'd been so happy growing up here. It was a great

town to be a kid in, quiet, friendly. Everyone knew everyone's business, but in a good way. Children felt safe, protected. She remembered riding her bike all over town, her parents never having to worry for her safety. She smiled at the memory. She didn't know many adults who could claim they'd had a happy childhood.

Then she wondered how much her happiness had had to do with the arrival of the Maconnals' new neighbors the summer she was ten.

She gripped the steering wheel tighter, but her eyes remained dry. She'd cried her last tears for Owen long ago, before the divorce. Her leaving had only been closure to a relationship that had dissipated long before.

"Dissipated." She said it aloud, liking the sound of the word. She loved words and she loved it when she discovered just the right word to describe something.

Dissipated was the perfect description of what had happened to her marriage. There had been no "other woman," no tragic death of a child, no shouting or slamming of doors. Nothing so dramatic or obvious. They had merely drifted apart. Their passion for each other, the excitement of the relationship had simply eased off until there was nothing there. It had faded as quietly and unobtrusively as beach erosion until the man who sat across from her at the breakfast table was a stranger.

Not that he had sat across the breakfast table from her often. When he had been in grad school, she had been the one absent. She'd worked crazy hours at the publishing house, leaving before Owen arose in the morning, often coming home long after he'd gone to bed. Then Owen landed a job with the prestigious Jacob & Jacob firm and he had begun working impossible hours, traveling to Europe, pulling all-nighters at the office.

Abby had tried to tell Owen how lonely she was, how much she missed him. She had even suggested he take a different job, one that paid less but demanded less as well. He had promised they would have children, that she would pursue her writing career. But Owen had insisted he was doing it all for her, *for them*. He kept promising they would have everything they wanted, once he was established in his field.

Abby had awakened one morning to realize she was thirty-three and nothing she had wanted out of life was in her future. She'd let herself out the door, leaving Owen a note and a phone number should he wish to discuss the separation. He hadn't called, and Abby had gone through with the divorce. Owen had been so civil through it all, so quiet, considerate, generous. She wished he had shouted, fought for her.

So, why was she back in Land's End now? She told Owen it was to pick up things she'd left in her parents' attic. And that was true. She wanted her high-school yearbook and her scrapbook. She wanted her collection of Laura Ingalls Wilder books she had been saving for the daughter she wondered now if she would ever have. She wanted the time capsule she and Owen had buried when they were fourteen.

But a part of her wanted to see Owen one more time. A final good-bye.

Abby shifted her old sedan into drive, signaled, and eased back onto the road. The sooner she got to the house, the sooner she could be on her way.

* * *

Owen tugged on the corner of the drape and peered out the window of the room the Maconnals had once called the front parlor in the big Victorian house. He wondered what time Abby had meant she would be here when she'd said Saturday afternoon. Early afternoon, like after twelve? Late afternoon, like four o'clock? Anything closer to five was early evening, wasn't it?

It was 3:30 and he was beginning to worry. What had started out as a summer storm off the southern tip of Florida had become a tropical storm east of the Peach State and, according to the local forecast, had just been updated to "Hurricane" status. Hurricane Alice was moving quickly up the coast, gaining speed and size by the hour. It was scheduled to hit the Virginia coast the following morning where it would either bounce off into the Atlantic or move inland straight for the Chesapeake Bay.

Owen watched a soda can roll across the street in front of his house. This wasn't the kind of weather to be traveling in. Where was Abby?

He'd been telling himself all day that he was just concerned for her safety. It wasn't that he wanted to see her. Why would he want to do that? If he saw her, talked to her, one thing would lead to another and the next thing he knew they'd be dredging up stuff that didn't need dredging. So what if he didn't really know why she left? What mattered was that she did. The marriage, the relationship, was long over and he was OK with that. He was a millennium kind of guy who knew two nice people could get a divorce and both still be nice people.

He *was* OK.

Owen spotted headlights, then a car moving down the street, and he tugged the curtain back a little farther. A pickup; it wasn't her. He let the curtain fall and walked to his desk, feeling silly. He ought to be doing something useful right now, like working.

He was turning "the front parlor" into a useful room. An office. He already had a desk with his computer, a drafting table and a filing cabinet. An old couch to lie on and mull over architectural designs would round out the space. He had only to make the purchase. He planned to take all the front parlor drapes down when he got a chance and let all that beautiful morning sunshine into his office. What did he care if anyone could see in at night? It wasn't as if he was going to be doing anything fun on the couch.

When Abby had left him, his friends had immediately urged him to begin dating, but he hadn't felt right about it. After all, according to the church, they were still married until the divorce was final. But even after the divorce, he just hadn't had any interest in seeing anyone else. First, his friends in Boston had tried to set up blind dates. When he refused, saying he needed more time, they shook their heads and muttered behind closed doors. Eventually they teased him outright. Some accused him of still being in love with his ex-wife. Others said he needed counseling. One associate had even suggested he might be gay, and that he should search out his true feelings, perhaps try dating a few men. Owen hadn't left because of the constant badgering, but it had certainly made it easier to walk out the door.

Now he was home in Land's End. Home with Zack and Ben. He studied his sketches of the McClusky house pinned on a bulletin board above his desk. He was proud of those initial sketches, proud of his work. Work felt good again. A job he enjoyed, good friends . . . Zack and Ben were right, he didn't need a woman in his life again. None of them did.

That was why he hadn't told—actually more like hadn't bothered to mention to—the guys that Abby was stopping by. Her visit was inconsequential, not worth the trouble of mentioning. It wasn't even a visit really.

He laughed aloud at his irrational rationalization. Was he losing it, or what?

His dog, Edgar, loped into the room and Owen offered a hand to scratch him between the ears. The dog immediately dropped on top of Owen's feet, basically nailing him to the floor with one hundred and four pounds of Bernese Mountain dog.

"Hey, get off."

Edgar lifted his head and looked up with big brown eyes. He licked the toe of Owen's sneaker.

"Move," Owen said again. "You big oaf."

The dog rolled over, off his master's feet, baring his spotted belly to be rubbed. Owen stood on one foot and scratched the big baby with the bottom of his shoe. "How's that? Feel good, boy?"

The dog's leg jiggled with pleasure.

Owen heard Abby's footsteps on the front porch even before she rang the bell.

Funny how a person could recognize another person's footsteps. God, how many times had he heard her walk across this porch? How many times had he crossed the porch with her? At first, just as friends, later as bashful girlfriend and boyfriend, and eventually lovers.

Now what were they? Exes. What a lousy word for two people who had spent so much of their life together. Abby was his ex—as if he could cross her out the way he crossed out a door or a window he placed wrong in a blueprint.

Owen opened the door as the chimes rang.

And there she was.

Abby was wet from the run from the car in the rain. Her straight blond hair stuck to her cheeks. Her white T-shirt was damp and clung to her skin, showing the perfect outline of her perfect breasts in her bra, which he guessed was wet, too.

"Owen," she said softly.

He stared at her, knowing his mouth had dropped open. He forcibly lifted his jaw to close it and not appear to be the complete ex-husband doofus that he was.

Had Abby always been this beautiful? Maybe she'd done something with her hair, colored it. Maybe she'd lost weight. Gained it? It had been only six months since the last time he saw her. Surely he would have remembered if she'd looked this good then.

"Can . . . can I come in?" she asked from the front porch, shaking water off her bare arms.

He stepped back. "Sure. Sorry. You're really wet. Must really be coming down out there, huh?"

He moved back far enough for her to step onto the painted jute carpet in the front hall. He reached around her and pushed the door shut. He felt so awkward, so off-kilter and nervous.

Edgar lumbered in and thrust his head beneath her hand to be petted.

"Hey there, Edgar. How's my boy? How's my big baby boy?" Abby squatted to hug the dog they had once both called their own. Edgar panted and chuffed with the excitement of seeing Abby again.

Leave it to a dog to break the ice.

By the time Abby stood again, Owen felt more level-headed. He had known it would be weird to see her, but it hadn't occurred to him that it would be this weird.

Damn . . . he missed her so much. He hadn't realized it until this moment.

"You want some tea?" He gestured toward the kitchen, then stuffed his hand into his jeans pocket because he didn't know what else to do with it. This was worse than the summer he was fourteen and realized he had a crush on her. "I can put some on."

She half-smiled, her blue eyes avoiding his. "Tea would be good."

He could tell she felt awkward, too. Maybe she was wishing she hadn't come, but just had him mail her stuff instead. He hoped not.

"And hey." He indicated her wet clothes. "Want to change? You're soaked. You'll be cold in a minute."

"Yeah, I guess I should. I've got dry things in the car." She pointed over her shoulder.

Through the large oval glass inset in the door he saw her blue sedan from their college days in the circular drive. He'd been telling her for years that she needed a new car. He'd offered to buy her one when they were still married. But she'd said she was attached to it, that it reminded her of a happy time in her life.

He had never felt that sad until this moment. Their college days had been happy, but eventually they had both become unhappy . . . hadn't they? Unhappy with each other, with the lives they had chosen.

"Let me run out and get your clothes for you," he said, as if he could make up for all he had done wrong by running the errand. The trouble was that he didn't know what he'd done wrong. She hadn't told him and he'd been too proud to ask. Too hurt. Now it was too late.

"I'm already wet," she argued. "No sense in both of us getting wet."

"You go up and get a warm shower. I'll get your clothes." He started for the door, before she could put up further argument.

"OK," Abby said softly as the door closed behind him.

She let her hands fall to her sides as she stared at the staircase with its acorn finial. Little seemed different in the house. Same chairs on the front porch. Same curtains in the windows. The walls of the papered hallway were still the vine and floral pattern she had helped her mother hang the summer she was seventeen.

She missed her mom. Her father had died while she was still in high school. Cancer. But it was her mother's death two years ago that had really left an ache in her heart. It was her mother who encouraged her to be a writer, and it bothered her that she'd never realized that dream before her mother passed away.

It was her mother's death that had made her realize she and Owen were never going to make it. She'd known then that he wasn't going to change, and she wasn't going to change her expectations. She wasn't going to give up her dream for his. The marriage had failed and she was willing to take the blame and move on.

She had sold Owen the house to help realize her dream of becoming a novelist. At the time of the divorce settlement he said he would buy the house as an investment. It had never occurred to her that he might actually move in. It never occurred to her that the renowned architect

and world traveler Owen Thomas might return to Land's
End to live. Had she known he was going to move into
her parents' home, she doubted she would ever have sold
it to him.

Abby slipped out of her soggy tennis shoes. She
couldn't believe how wet she had gotten just running from
the car. The storm had seemed to increase in size and
power as she passed into the town limits. She smiled
wryly, wondering if the storm was a reflection of what
she was feeling inside. She left her shoes by the door and
shook her finger at Edgar. "Leave it," she warned.

The dog looked up at her with innocent eyes and
chuffed softly.

She padded across the hall and up the steps, her damp
socks making a squishing sound on the polished hardwood
floor. Upstairs, she passed the first door on the right—her
old bedroom—and took the second on the right to the
master bath.

Abby couldn't resist smiling as she entered the bathroom. A pile of wet towels lay on the floor where Owen
had left them. Some things never changed.

She let out a sigh. She was beginning to chill and goose-
bumps rose on her forearms. Owen was right, she needed
a warm shower.

But then Owen was always right. It had been so difficult
to argue with a man who was always right. So hard to live
with a man who was always right, when she was a woman
who wasn't.

Abby glanced at the door she'd left partially open. The
more she thought about a warm shower, the colder she
felt. But she hadn't heard Owen come in from outside yet,
and he had her dry clothes.

She glanced at the claw-footed Victorian bathtub with its shower curtain drawn back enticingly. Should she get in and hope he would leave her clothes outside the door, or did she wait for him to come in from outside?

Abby didn't like the thought of standing naked in Owen's bathroom, having to ask for her clothes. She didn't like the idea of feeling so vulnerable, but she didn't like the idea of catching cold either.

"This is ridiculous," she said aloud, catching a glance of herself in the mirror. She looked like a wet rat. No wonder he'd left her. Then she remembered and smiled to herself again. That's right—she'd left him.

Abby stripped off her wet T-shirt, and tossed it onto the pile of discarded towels. She added her bra, shorts and panties to the pile and climbed into the tub.

I won't cry, she thought. *What reason would I possibly have to cry? The marriage is over, the relationship is over, but I survived.*

But she couldn't stop herself.

Behind the wall of the curtain she allowed the warm rain of the shower to pour over her face and wash away the tears of her mixed emotions. She hadn't realized how hard it was going to be to come home. No, it wasn't the house. It wasn't even the fact that her mother and father were dead and she was alone in the world. It was Owen. Her tears were for the love she had lost and the hopelessness of the love she still felt for Owen.

Three

Owen stood outside the bathroom door, Edgar on his heels. Abby's overnight bag swung on his elbow. He heard the shower running and hesitated. Should he open the door and put the bag on the floor or should he just leave it in the hall and retreat downstairs to the kitchen?

It seemed silly to leave someone's clothes in the hall, but he didn't want to overstep any boundaries. He wasn't sure of the rules of being an ex-husband. He grimaced. Apparently he hadn't been sure of the rules of being a husband either, else he would have done a better job.

"What do you think, boy?" Owen whispered.

The dog stared at his owner, then at the door. It was slightly ajar.

"That's what I was thinking. The door's open a crack—she must have left it open so I could put her clothes inside, right?" He frowned. "Because we both know it's not an invitation, don't we?"

The dog cocked his head.

Owen made a move for the door, then stopped. "Tell her? Don't tell her?"

The dog chuffed.

"Right. Don't tell her. Leave her to take her shower in peace. She'll know I brought up the clothes when she sees the bag."

Owen pushed the door open a little farther so that he could place the small duffel just inside. But like all the other doors in the house built at the turn of the century, this door was unpredictable. He pushed it open eight inches, and it kept right on going.

"Ah, hell," he muttered as it swung out of reach, not stopping until it hit the door jam. Now he would have to step inside the bathroom to close the door again. Inside with his ex-wife . . . his naked ex-wife.

He took one step.

"Owen, that you?" Abby called from the shower.

He glanced up without thinking. He didn't mean to look. He'd had no intentions of looking.

But through the filmy shower curtain he caught a glimpse of her profile as she turned toward the open door. He immediately felt his face grow warm. His boxers beneath his jeans seemed to shrink. It didn't matter that he couldn't actually see her. This almost seemed worse. Just an outline of her rounded hips, flat belly, perfectly shaped jutting breasts, her chin he had once loved to kiss.

She was so beautiful that she took his breath away.

He swallowed hard. "Sorry," he said, trying to sound as casual as possible. "Edgar knocked open the door." He backed up. "Your bag's on the floor." He closed the door behind him and leaned against it.

"Sorry, boy." He patted the dog between his ears. "Didn't mean to blame you for something you didn't do, but I didn't want her thinking I was a pervert or anything.

Let's get downstairs before we get into any more trouble, huh?"

By the time Abby climbed out of the shower, dried off and dressed, she was feeling better. She'd had her little cry and now she was fine. Just fine. She would have a cup of tea, get what she wanted out of the attic, and be on her way south.

Carrying a hand towel to finish drying her hair, she found Owen in the kitchen. He had brewed fresh hot tea. Her favorite.

"Feel better?" he asked, his back to her as he removed mugs from a cabinet.

"Much, thanks. And thanks for getting my clothes." She took one of the kitchen chairs, running the small white towel over her head.

He brought the mug to the table. "Storm's getting worse."

She glanced out the window above the sink, surprised by how violently the old lilac bush outside was swaying. "Wow. The wind's really picking up."

"They expect the hurricane to hit somewhere by morning."

"Hurricane?" She glanced up at him, taken back. "There's a hurricane coming?"

"Haven't you been listening to the news?" Owen carried the blue and white striped teapot to the table and took the chair across from her at the oak dining table. As kids, they had once made peanut butter and jelly sandwiches together at this table.

She shook her head. "Radio in the car doesn't work. I've been listening to a book tape."

He poured the steaming dark Assum tea, first for her, then himself. "That tropical storm from earlier in the week became a hurricane. It may hit here by midday tomorrow."

She stared dismally at the window again. She could see the elm tree branches beyond the lilac bush swaying through the rain-splattered glass. "Not great for traveling," she said in a small voice. She felt silly. How could she have set off in the middle of a hurricane? She should have checked the weather before she left Boston. But she'd been so anxious to get on the road and on with her life that it hadn't occurred to her.

"I think you'd better stay put for the night," Owen said, bringing sugar and fresh lemon to the table.

She frowned, spooning sugar from the bowl into her cup. "Great. I was hoping to drive straight through and save on the cost of a hotel."

He looked up at her. She had forgotten how attractive Owen was with his short-cropped blond hair and blue eyes a girl could lose herself in. It didn't matter that he hadn't shaved this morning; she always liked a little blond beard stubble.

And he was being so attentive, hanging on her every word. The last few months they had been married she didn't think he had heard a single word she'd said. She had been surprised that he'd even noticed she was gone.

"Hotel? You don't need to stay in a hotel," he said. "Stay here."

She glanced down at her tea, stirring it into a whirlpool with her spoon. "No. Owen, that's not a good idea. I . . ."

"Don't be ridiculous," he interrupted. "This used to be

your house. For heaven's sake, Abby, you can sleep in your old room. Hook up your laptop and get a little work done this evening if you want. I won't bother you."

She glanced at the window again. The thought was tempting. She honestly didn't want to spend money on a hotel room. And he was right. This had been her house before it was his. If anyone had a right to stay, it was her. She looked back at him, uncertain. Staying here wasn't in her plans, and staying with Owen certainly wasn't. But a hurricane wasn't in her plans, either. "You certain it won't make you uncomfortable?" she asked. "Me being here?"

"What?" He spread his arms wide. "I'm going to see you in your underwear or something? Abby, we were married for ten years. I think I can control myself."

She lowered her head with a faint smile. "You're right."

"So, you'll stay?"

He almost sounded excited. Pleased. She had to work hard to lose the smile. "I'll stay. But—" She held up one finger, lifting her gaze to meet his. "Only if you'll let me cook supper—to pay you back. It is your house now—you paid for it."

He grinned. "Deal." He lifted his cup to his lips. She remembered he liked his tea with lots of sugar and milk. "What do you want to make? I'll run to the store before it gets too bad out."

"You don't have to do that. I'll just throw something together from what you have around the house." In a way she felt strange, as if she were talking to a stranger. They were being so polite to each other, so kind. But in another way it felt good. In the last days of their crumbling marriage there had been no comfortable small talk, just the essentials; who had fed Edgar, who would pick up the dry cleaning, where they were meeting Friday night for cocktails. She had missed this kind of talk at the kitchen table.

"Make something from here, will you?" His eyes twinkled as he jumped out of his chair and pulled open the refrigerator door. "Let's see. I have mustard, mayo, relish, half a stick of butter." He reached in and lifted the cover of a pizza box. "Pizza crusts, two Mexican beers, and . . . half a gallon of milk." He turned. "What can you make from that?"

"What about the freezer?" She couldn't resist a smile of amusement.

He pulled it open. "Ice, peas and . . . butter pecan ice cream."

"OK," she agreed, pouring herself more tea. "Go to the grocery store. Edgar and I will hold down the fort."

He tossed a notepad and pen. "Make me a list. Your wish is my command."

After Owen left with her list to make shrimp scampi, she wandered about the house, running her fingers over the furniture, most of which had belonged to her parents. At the time of the divorce, when she sold Owen the house, he had promised she could come back for any of the furnishing she wished. He was a bachelor with no need for Victorian antiques. But the rose side tables in the living room, the mirrored coat rack in the entryway, even the oak kitchenette belonged here. She couldn't imagine the furnishings anywhere else.

Little seemed different in the house, save for the smells. When her mother had been alive it had always smelled of lemon furniture polish and breakfast, lunch or dinner. Her mom had been a terrific cook. Now it smelled . . . empty.

At the parlor door, Abby halted. She hadn't peeked into the bedrooms upstairs yet, but this was the one room Owen had changed. This room looked like him. He had removed all the furniture that had previously been here and set his drafting table against the west wall. He had an old tin two-drawer filing cabinet and the desk they had bought together at the import shop. He had taken the area carpets up to bare the natural beauty of the hardwood floor. She could see where he had begun to strip the floral wallpaper. Two gallons of white paint rested on oilcloth in the corner of the room.

She had to smile as she leaned against the arched doorway and crossed her arms over her chest. Yes, this was Owen. Owen was spatial. He liked lots of room to think.

Abby was irritated by the twinge she felt in her chest. She had been telling herself for the last few months that she was over Owen. She had been certain she was ready to move on. Now, being here, seeing him—he was being so damned nice, the way she remembered him.

The phone rang and without thinking she walked to the desk and picked it up. "Hello."

"Hello?"

She thought she recognized the male voice, but it wasn't Owen. "Yes?" she said.

"Um," said the puzzled caller. "Is Owen there?"

Only then did she realize who it was. Ben. Handsome, charming Bennett Gordon. "Ben," she said with a smile.

"Who is this?"

She slid into Owen's chair. Edgar wandered into the room and slid to the floor at her feet. "It's Abby."

"Abby?"

She picked up a mechanical pencil to doodle on Owen's desk blotter. "Blast from the past, huh?"

"Abby, what the hell are you doing there?"

"Nice to talk to you, too, Ben." She had always liked Ben and gotten along with him just fine. Maybe because she'd never been interested in him romantically. Every girl in Land's End had been in love with Ben when they were in high school. He'd dated practically every one of them, and broken their hearts, too.

"I'm sorry, I . . . I'm just surprised to hear your voice, that's all."

"I understand." As she spoke she wrote her name. Only after she'd scrawled it did she realize she'd mistakenly written Abby Thomas. She wasn't Abby Thomas anymore; she had taken back her maiden name as part of the divorce settlement. She scratched out Thomas and wrote Maconnal in scrawling cursive. "I was just teasing you."

"So, um, out of curiosity, what *are* you doing there?"

"You never could stand not to know what was going on, could you?" She wrote her name again this time correctly. She liked to practice for the day when she would have to autograph her books. "I came by to pick up a few things. I'm moving to Myrtle Beach."

"I see. And Owen's not there?"

"No. He went to the grocery store. He didn't have anything for dinner."

"So, you're staying for dinner."

She turned in the swiveling chair to look out the windows that faced east and looked over the front porch onto the street. The wind was still blowing like a gale. "Dinner and the night." She turned back in her chair to her doodling. "The storm. Owen says it's turned into a hurricane.

I didn't think I'd better be driving into a hurricane in that old jalopy of mine."

"So, you're spending the night?"

"Ben?" She knitted her brows. He was acting awfully strange. "Why do you keep repeating everything I say?"

"Could you, um, just tell Owen I called. Tell him to give me a ring as soon as he gets in, will you?"

"Sure. Nice talking to you, Ben."

"Good to talk to you, too."

"Bye." She hung up the phone and reached down to give Edgar a rub on the head. "That was so weird," she muttered, shaking her head. Then she decided she'd better call her girlfriend Jess in Boston and let her know where she was. It was Jess's family who owned the cottage in Myrtle Beach.

Jess didn't pick up and the answering machine came on. "This is Jessica. You know what to do." *Beeeep*.

Abby could never resist a chuckle when she heard Jess's message. The woman was just so practical. It was why they could be such good friends. Abby was the romantic, the dreamer, while Jess was the one who kept her feet on the floor.

"Jess, it's me, Abby. I just wanted you to know that I'm in Land's End. There's a bad storm coming through so I'm going to spend the night at Owen's. The number is—"

Abby heard a click as someone picked up the phone. "You're staying the night at Owen's? Are you out of your tree?"

"So, you are home." Abby wrapped the phone cord around her finger.

"Pretending I'm out on a date with a handsome virile

male while I'm actually highlighting my hair with the cat for company."

Abby laughed.

"So, please tell me the ex is not there. He's out of town on a business trip or on his way to hell, right?"

"Jess!"

"Tell me it ain't so."

"He's here. But it's fine. He offered to let me stay here because the weather is too bad to drive in."

"I'm sure he did. Offer you his side of the bed, too?"

"It's not like that," Abby defended. "He's been really sweet."

"Men usually are when they're trying to get you in the sack."

"Is that the only thing you ever think of?" Abby questioned with pseudo-disgust.

"Hey, I've got an ex, remember? The divorce was barely cold and he was sniffing at my door."

"Well, there's been no sniffing. Owen's been nothing but nice. I'm only staying until morning, noon at the latest, until the storm passes and then I'll be on my way."

"You say he's being good?"

She smiled. "Very sweet and attentive. He went out to the car in the rain to get my clothes for me, and he made me tea."

"You took off your clothes for him and he paid you with a cup of tea? Cheap date."

"I'm hanging up now," Abby said good-naturedly. "I just wanted you to know I was OK. I'll call you when I get to Myrtle Beach."

"I'm just warning you now. This is ex-syndrome you're experiencing. First he's being sweet, you fall into bed with him and then next thing you know you're hating his guts and your own as well . . . again."

"Hanging up," Abby said sweetly. "Hanging up now."

"Don't do it, Abby. Save yourself!" Jess declared dramatically. "Run. Run into the night, into the storm."

"It's a hurricane."

"Even a hurricane is better than an ex-husband on the prowl."

"Bye, Jess." Abby hung up the phone with a chuckle. "Can you believe her?" she asked her faithful companion.

Edgar lifted his massive head from his paws and stared up at her with big brown eyes.

Abby was just getting up from Owen's desk when she heard him run up the front porch steps. She met him at the door. "You're soaked!"

He handed her several plastic sacks with the local food store imprint on them. "It is really coming down now."

She stepped back to let him in. He kicked his sneakers off and left them beside hers. "Can you get the groceries?" he asked. "I'm going to run up and change."

"No problem. I told you," she said heading for the kitchen. "Edgar and I have everything under control."

Abby was just emptying the last bag when Owen came into the kitchen. He had changed into khaki shorts and an orange polo shirt. Abby never liked orange on men, but it always looked good on Owen, especially when he was as suntanned as he was now.

"Need help?"

Abby remembered how much they had enjoyed cooking in the kitchen together when they had first married. It had been years now since they'd done this and again she was hit by a wave of nostalgia. "You can start peeling garlic." She tossed him heads of garlic.

"Goody, my favorite." He caught all three in the air and then tossed one after the other up, juggling them.

"I'm sure your parents are impressed with all the money they put into your college education so that you could learn how to juggle."

Grinning, he caught the garlic bulbs one by one and set them on the counter. He pulled a chopping block from a cabinet below. "You used to like it when I juggled."

"I used to like when you did a lot of things . . ." The words were out of her mouth before she realized it and no matter what she did, she knew she couldn't take them back. She glanced over at him to see him looking down at the cloves in front of him. Her comment had hurt him. She could see it in the tight lines around his mouth.

"I'm sorry," she said quietly. "That wasn't fair."

"No. Fair and justified." He lifted his chin to meet her gaze. "Abby, if there was any way we could go back. If I could just—"

She shook her head, interrupting him. "Owen, please. Don't. Let's just have a nice evening and not talk about any of that." She knew her eyes pleaded with him. "Please?"

She thought he was going to say something more, but he didn't. His frown was replaced by a tight grin. "All right. If that's what you want."

For some reason her heart was pounding. She should have known better than to have agreed to stay tonight. Jess was right. This was a bad idea. "It's what I want," she said firmly.

He gave a nod and picked up a glass to strike the garlic head and separate the cloves.

The doorbell rang and Abby leaned back to see who it was. The kitchen door was a straight shot to the front door. She noted with amusement who the visitors were. "Ah, I think you've got company," she told Owen, crossing the kitchen to put the shrimp in the fridge until she was ready for it.

"Who?" He wiped his hands on a kitchen towel.

"Your buddies Curly and Mo, of course."

"Here? Now?"

"I didn't get a chance to tell you." She put the shrimp into the fridge. "Ben called a few minutes ago. Said you should call him right away."

"They know you're here?"

She looked at him oddly. "Well, I did answer your phone. I think they guessed I must be in the house."

Owen shook his head as he headed out of the kitchen. Ben and Zack were leaning against the doorbell now.

"Unbelievable," Owen muttered at he flung open the door. Then to his friends, "What do you think you're doing here?"

Four

"What do we think we're doing here?" Ben pulled him through the door, onto the porch. Zack closed it soundly behind him. "What are *you* doing here?"

"If you must know, I was juggling garlic before I was so rudely interrupted." Owen wrapped his arms around himself and shivered. Despite the overhang of the porch, he was getting wet. "You know it's raining out here? You'd think between the two of you with those fancy degrees of yours that you'd be able to figure out how to stay out of the rain."

Zack and Ben stood in front of him as if they were the firing squad, their faces entirely too serious.

"What's going on here, buddy? Talk to us," Ben urged.

"What do you mean, what's going on? I'm having dinner with an old friend." It came out more defensively than Owen had intended. He couldn't believe they were here checking up on him in the middle of this storm. He couldn't believe he felt as if he needed to defend himself. It was Abby for heaven's sake!

"An old friend?" Zack lifted an eyebrow. "You mean an old wife."

"Come on! What are you thinking here?" Ben tapped his temple. "That's a woman you've got in there. *A woman.*"

Owen opened his eyes wide, glanced over his shoulder through the window of the front door, then back at his buddies. "Ah, hell, you're right!" He feigned surprise, slapping his forehead. "She is a woman! What was I thinking?"

"Be serious here, man," Zack said.

Owen cracked an amused grin. If he stood out here much longer he was going to have to change his clothes again; it was raining sideways. Wind and rain were stripping leaves from the trees, hurling them across the porch, sending them spiraling with the ferocity of a wind tunnel. "You be serious! You guys are in a spin over nothing! Abby just stopped by to pick up some things on her way south. She's rented a cottage in Myrtle Beach. She's writing a novel, you know." He gestured. "It's just for one night, for cryin' out loud."

"She's not leaving tonight?" Zack was indignant.

"I told you she was staying," Ben said to Zack. "She said so on the phone."

Now they were talking about him as if he wasn't even there.

Owen glared at his two best friends who were soaked, too. "You two sound worse than the Spanish Inquisition."

"We are worse." Zack stuffed his hands into the pockets of his old corduroy surfer shorts. "We're Bachelors, Inc. Remember? We've sworn to uphold the laws of the organization."

"The by-laws of the GAG Club do not allow sleepovers

with women, Owen," Ben intoned. "Never did. Never will."

"You two are serious!"

"We all swore to look after each other. We're just here in your best interest."

"In a hurricane!"

"Come on, Owen." Ben touched Owen's wet arm. "You'd do the same for Zack or me. You'd be here in a hurricane for us, if we needed you, wouldn't you?"

"Of course I would. If you *needed* me." He shifted his weight from one bare foot to the other. He was getting cold now. "But I don't need you."

Ben glanced over Owen's shoulder, through the oval window in the door. "She's making you dinner?" Now he sounded like Friday on "Dragnet."

"Scampi. Then we're both going to work for a while. Then we're going to bed. *Separately,*" he emphasized. "With at least two closed doors and a pair of boxers between us. Then she'll be gone tomorrow as soon as this thing blows over." He tapped his forehead. "I can't believe I'm telling you all this. You guys are not my mother."

"Speaking of which, does your mom know she's here?" Ben glanced in the direction of their house. "I'm sure she wouldn't approve."

"You're just being a nice guy, huh?" Zack questioned. "Letting her stay the night here? You had no ulterior motives?"

"No." Owen was being honest when he said it. He didn't have ulterior motives. He hadn't to begin with, at least. He didn't have to admit to his buddies that he had just wanted to see her once more. He didn't have to tell them how nice it was to have her here, either. They wouldn't understand. How could they? Zack's ex-wife had been such a witch and Ben had never been married at all.

"Look, she's taken a leave of absence from her editing job to write and she's trying to watch her money," Owen explained. "What would be the sense in making her pay for a night in a hotel when this used to be her house? I couldn't ask her to do that."

Zack took his turn at peering through the glass. "You'd have been better off paying the hotel tab, bro. Way safer."

"Way safer," Ben agreed, watching her through the window. He squinted, wiping rain from his eyes. "She get her hair cut or something? She looks different—mighty fine for an ex-wife."

"Hey, you stay away from her." Owen thumped Ben on the chest. He was a notorious womanizer. Owen wouldn't trust him alone with his grandmother. "You have nothing to worry about. I haven't violated any GAG rules. I'm just helping out a friend."

"You're sure?" Ben's gaze met his.

"I'm sure." Owen turned back to the door. "Now go home, both of you, before you get blown off the porch."

"I think we'd better come in and say hi," Ben said. "Just to be sure."

"No. You don't need to—"

But Ben and Zack didn't pay any attention to him; they pushed past him, right into the house.

"Abby!" Ben called, throwing open his arms. He offered her his best boyish grin.

She appeared in the kitchen doorway.

"Look what I found on the front porch," Owen said, feeling a little silly. What was it about women that always made men feel a little foolish when they were with their friends?

"Looks like we've got two drowned rats." Abby smiled from the doorway, drying her hands on a towel. "You guys want to stay for supper? We've got plenty."

"No," Owen said firmly.

"Sure." Zack kicked off his docksiders in the entryway and headed for the kitchen, leaving a trail of wet footprints behind him.

"You bet," Ben echoed.

Abby smacked Zack on the backside with the kitchen towel as he went by her.

"Hey! What about me?" Ben halted in the archway. "Equal opportunity abuse?"

She grinned. "For you, lover-boy, a kiss." She lifted up on her toes and kissed his cheek.

Owen's hackles rose. Why were Ben and Zack getting all this attention? Abby certainly hadn't kissed him hello and hell, they'd slept together for a dozen years.

"Fine, you get a kiss. I get assaulted." Zack dug into a bag of baby carrots Abby had left on the counter for salad. He popped one into his mouth.

Owen stood in the doorway, feeling like an outsider in his own kitchen. Abby didn't seem nearly as easygoing alone with him as she did with them.

Can I blame her?

"I'll peel the shrimp," Owen said needing something to do with his hands.

"Would you?"

The smile she offered was hesitant, barely a smile, but it overwhelmed him. At this moment he thought he would have peeled enough shrimp for scampi for all of Land's End, if she'd asked him.

Owen smiled back and their gazes met.

Abby felt a strange warmth on the back of her neck as Owen looked at her from across the kitchen. What was she getting all giddy about? It wasn't as if he'd offered to slay a dragon for her or anything so romantic as that. It was two pounds of shrimp, for heaven's sake. This was Owen, not a potential date. Owen. Her ex. She had to keep reminding herself of that.

She turned away and went back to making the salad.

Abby whipped up her scampi and the four of them sat down at her mom's old round Victorian oak table to share in the feast. The wind was howling outside like a gale, but inside, among friends, the kitchen was warm and cozy. The conversation was relaxed as the three men, who had been constants in her life when she was growing up, exchanged easy banter.

Abby enjoyed the meal as she hadn't enjoyed one in a long time. It felt so good to be back in Land's End, here in her parents' kitchen. It felt good to be with the guys again.

Abby glanced over her iced-tea glass at Owen. He and Ben were in heated discussion over the changes in the Orioles bullpen. Discussing sports had always been one of their favorite pastimes though it was more like arguing over sports.

Watching Owen, listening to him, painfully reminded her of why she had fallen in love with him in the first place. Certainly he was handsome, intelligent, a good conversationalist. But Ben and Zack were all that, too. Owen was different. He had a certain sparkle in his eyes that the other two didn't. He seemed to enjoy life so much, appreciate every moment. At least, that was the way he used to be, and seemed to be again, now that they were divorced.

Abby had replayed the events of the last two years over and over in her mind as she packed to head for the Carolinas. Had she done the right thing in leaving Owen? She'd told herself she had. She'd told herself she just couldn't live that way any longer. But seeing him like this, laughing, smiling made her realize how desperately she missed him. Missed the old Owen, not the man she had divorced.

"Hey, Owen." Ben scraped the bottom of the scampi bowl. "Did Zack tell you about our team?"

"Your team?" Owen poured her fresh iced tea, then topped off his own glass.

He had always been so considerate.

"Our baseball team!"

"You guys are playing baseball? Aren't you a little old for that kind of thing?"

"Not us," Zack joined in. "We're coaching boys' teams."

Owen glanced sideways at Abby and winked conspiratorially.

He could be so damned charming when he wanted to be, too.

"Coach? You guys? You've got to be kidding."

"It's for the Kid's League. We've both got teams—have a little friendly competition going on." Ben jerked his thumb in Zack's direction. "I'm betting my team will beat Zack's and come out on top at the end of the season."

Owen glanced at Zack. "And how does Savannah feel about you coaching boys and not her team?"

Zack grinned proudly. "Her team *is* the boy's team."

"Good for her," Abby injected.

"So, how about you, Owen?" Ben wiped his mouth with a napkin from a taco joint. "They could still use some help. You were always the best player of the three of us. The league is desperate for volunteers."

"I don't know," Owen hedged.

Abby turned to him. "I think you ought to do it. You'd be great with little boys."

"A great drill sergeant," Zack commented. "He'd have those eight-year-olds whipped into shape in no time. Make men out of them!"

"I'm not so sure that would be a good idea." Owen folded his napkin, attempting to make some sort of origami bird. "I get high-strung at times."

"You?" Abby couldn't resist amused sarcasm. "Not you, Owen."

Zack and Ben burst into hearty male laughter.

"Hey, where's my support here, buddies?" Owen stared at them incredulously. "A guy is supposed to be able to depend on his friends to lift him up, not tear him down."

Still chuckling, Abby nudged Owen. "Seriously, I think you should volunteer to coach a team. You'd be great. No one knows as much about baseball as you do. And it would be good for your new company," she added. "You know how people can be around here. You should show them that you're willing to add something to the community, not just take people's money." She rose to begin clearing away the dirty dishes.

"Let me do this." Owen took her plate from her. "Better

yet, let them." He dropped her plate on top of Ben's. "They're the ones who came to dinner uninvited."

"I beg your pardon. Abby invited us." Zack climbed out of his chair, taking his plate with him.

"You really think I could coach eight-year-olds?" Owen asked her.

Abby eased back into her chair. "Absolutely. I wouldn't say so if I didn't mean it. If there's one thing you can say about me, it's that I was always honest with you."

The moment the words were out of her mouth, she regretted them. She hadn't meant to bring their personal relationship into the conversation. It just slipped. But as her gaze met his, she was surprised by the emotion she saw. Could that really be pain? Regret? She didn't know what she had expected when she came to Land's End, but this wasn't it.

He missed her. She could see it in his eyes.

Abby turned away and caught Ben watching them. He had seen the exchange between her and Owen and he didn't appear to approve. So, it couldn't be her imagination, could it? Owen did miss her.

I need to get out of here, Abby thought with a silent groan. *I didn't come here for this. It's too late for regrets and second guessing myself. Way too late.*

Owen got out of his chair and started loading the dishwasher. "All right, I'll do it," he said firmly. "I'll call the league in the morning and volunteer."

Abby stood, taking her tea with her. "Well, if you guys have KP duty under control, I'm going upstairs. I have some things to go through in the attic." She nodded to Zack and Ben. "Good to see you guys."

"You too, Abby," Ben said. "Call me."

She laughed. "Yeah, right. Dream on, Bennett."

"Good to see you again," Zack said warmly. He gave a little wave.

Without a word to Owen, Abby slipped out of the kitchen and climbed the stairs to the attic.

The minute Abby was out of the kitchen, Ben was at Owen's side. "Dangerous," he breathed, shaking his head. "I'm telling you, this is dangerous, Owen."

"What?" He pretended innocence and went on loading the dishes.

"You know what. Having her here. Spending the night." Zack came up on the other side of him.

They had him surrounded.

"You guys are making a mountain out of a molehill." Owen added a plate, facing it toward the center of the washer the way Abby liked it done. "There's nothing between us anymore." He threw up one hand in disgust. "Shoot, she wouldn't have me for anything after the hell I put her through."

Zack and Ben exchanged glances.

"Remember, she left you," Ben said. "Don't fall for those big blue eyes of hers or that tan. She *left* you. Packed her bags and mailed the divorce papers."

"Can you blame her, considering the way I acted? That last year before she left . . ." Owen shook his head in disgust as he recalled. "It was as if she didn't even exist. I don't know what came over me. I wanted to make partner so badly that—" He exhaled. "I lost sight of what mattered to me. Worse, I lost sight of what mattered to her."

"Owen, listen to yourself." Ben grabbed both of his

arms and gave him a shake. "You're making excuses for her."

Owen met Ben's gaze, warning him to back off, and Ben dropped his hands. "I won't stand to have you say anything against her. I owe her that much at least."

"I'm not saying anything against her," Ben said quietly. "I'm just reminding you of the facts. I'm thinking of you. We know how much you were hurt when she left, even if you don't."

The room was quiet for a moment, except for the sound of the wind blowing outside and the scratch of branches on the window.

"I appreciate your concern," Owen said finally. He started loading the dishwasher again. "But it's just like I told you. She's spending the night and then she's leaving tomorrow."

"You could come bunk at my house if you wanted to," Zack offered. He smiled, trying to make light of a conversation that had become entirely too heavy. "Savannah would love a sleepover."

"And hey, you know you can always stay with Dad and me."

Owen lined the dirty glasses up on the top rack of the dishwasher. "I appreciate the offer, but I think I can control my bestial desires, gentlemen."

"You telling us to hit the road?" Zack lifted a blond eyebrow. "Because if that's what you're saying, you just have to come out and say it."

Owen glanced up. "Hit the road, guys. I'm a big boy. I can take care of myself."

"All right." Ben slapped his shoulder. "We'll go, but you call us if you need us. She comes slithering down the steps in some kind of slinky nightie, you call us. You hear me?"

Owen laughed and threw a hand over his head as the two of them left the kitchen. "Drive safely."

"Talk to you tomorrow," Ben hollered.

"Tomorrow."

Owen heard the front door close and he and Abby were alone in the house again. He took his time rinsing the dishes, loading the dishwasher, putting everything away.

As he worked, he thought about Abby sorting through her belongings in the attic. The more he thought about her, the more he wanted to be up there with her. Call it crazy, but having dinner with her like this reminded him of all the reasons why he had fallen in love with her in the fourth grade. She was so bright and articulate, so fun and full of life. People were always surprised when they'd met him and Abby and found out they'd been a couple since junior high. Maybe it did sound a little unbelievable, but it was true. And the fact of the matter was that Abby Maconnal had made Owen what he was. And no matter how hard he had tried, he had not felt like himself since Abby had left him.

He closed the dishwasher, started it up, and leaned against it.

Edgar wandered into the room, checked out his empty food bowl and came to sit at Owen's feet.

Owen absently scratched the dog behind his ears. So, now what?

He was man enough to say he'd screwed up big time. He had thought he could live without Abby, but he couldn't. Not and be whole. She was as much a part of him as his arm, or his drafting table in the other room. No matter what his well-meaning friends said, he knew he needed her and he suspected she still needed him.

The question was, was he man enough to try to get her back?

Five

Abby sat cross-legged on an old rolled up rug and flipped through a scrapbook of photos and mementos from her school days. There were pictures of her and her girlfriends clamming down on the bay. A picture of her in her softball uniform, wearing Owen's team hat. A movie stub from a show she and Owen had seen when they were in high school, a picture of the two of them in their prom clothes after the prom. Owen was missing his tie and jacket; she was barefoot. They both looked so happy.

She flipped through the pages, smiling and chuckling as she recalled certain events. She remembered the math league finals and how she had beaten Owen. He'd been angry with her for days and pretended not to be. She remembered when he had received his Eagle Scout award; the program was folded up and stuck between the pages of the album. She had been so proud of him.

Turning the pages, revisiting her past, made her realize that divorcing Owen and moving away from him wasn't going to take him out of her life. He had been so much a part of what she became. And no matter how hard she tried not to, she couldn't help but smile at that thought. Owen had always brought out the best in her. He had encouraged her to try out for the lead in the senior production, the part she got. In college, he insisted she play rugby. He convinced her to take classes that interested her even when they weren't on the requirement list for her major. Owen had taught her how to experience life. How to enjoy it to its fullest.

She heard footsteps on the attic stairs and wiped at her eyes that must have grown damp from the dust.

"Hey," Owen said from the top of the stairs.

"Hey, yourself." She didn't look up, but concentrated on the scrapbook in her lap.

"Find what you were looking for?"

She lifted one shoulder. "It's not that any of this stuff is valuable, I just wanted it."

"Of course it's valuable!" He came into the attic, ducking where the ceiling was low. "How could you live without this?" He picked up a dusty bowler hat from a box and dropped it onto his head. He looked utterly ridiculous . . . and utterly irresistible.

Sheesh, she thought. Maybe Jess was right, maybe she did need a roll in the hay.

"Give me that. That was my dad's." She put out her hand, but he wouldn't give it up. She refused to give him the satisfaction of getting into a tug of war with him. "I really need to pack up most of this junk and give it to the church for their next yard sale," she said, not really meaning it.

"What you got there?" He came closer, glancing down at the scrapbook in her lap.

"Just some old pictures. More junk."

She started to close up the book, but he dropped down on the plywood subfloor beside her and caught the cover before it closed. "Any pictures of me in there?"

"Found one of you with a crewcut," she teased.

"You did not! Give me that." He slid the book from her lap so that it rested halfway on his. His bare knee rested against hers. "I wouldn't have been caught dead with a crewcut."

"Apparently you would when you were eleven." She flipped to the page and pointed.

"Oh, god," he moaned. "I can't believe you let me go on living, looking like that."

She laughed and turned the page. "Remember this?" She pointed to a napkin folded into a bird and pressed flat to fit into the book.

His forehead creased. "I make it?"

"Made it for me when you were at Boy Scout Camp after sixth grade."

"We learned important skills in Boy Scout Camp."

"Right," she snickered. "I remember. You always got to go to Boy Scout Camp and I got stuck in Girl Scout Camp. I learned how to sew on stupid buttons and you got to learn how to burp your ABCs."

He looked at her. They were so close that she could feel his breath on her cheek. "If you're really still that upset over it, I can try to teach you. You know what they say, Ab, you're never too old to learn something new."

Her shoulder was against his. "No, thank you. I think I've grown out of that, although I'm not so sure I can say the same for the members of the GAG Club."

He looked hurt. "What? They were well-behaved at supper. No one said or did anything outrageous."

"I know." She began to turn the pages again. There were some things that she had no clue what their significance was. A straw paper, a square of blue cloth, a matchbook cover from the Pizza Palace. "It's just that the three of you still stick together like you did when you were kids. All those private jokes, it's just so weird when you're an outsider."

"You're not an outsider," he said quietly.

"No, well, Zack and Ben think I am now. They didn't appreciate finding me here."

"So. I appreciate you being here."

She could feel him looking at her. She wanted to turn her head, to meet his gaze, but she didn't dare. Her feelings were so jumbled. She hadn't come here expecting to feel this way about Owen. The sense of loss was almost overwhelming. He was such a damned nice guy and she'd blown it. At the very least she'd allowed him to blow it.

Owen was silent for a moment, looking at her. "What's this?"

She smiled as she looked down at the piece of folded paper. She didn't have to look at it to know what it was. It was a love poem she had written for Owen in her freshman year in college. She had never shown it to him. Funny that she would keep it.

"None of your business." She turned the page and pointed. "Look, you and the guys on the hood of my car down on the beach. We were seniors in college that summer. Remember?"

He shook his head. "We looked so young."

She turned the page again. "I take it Zack and Ben are gone. They didn't feel the need to camp out on the living room floor tonight and protect you from the evil divor-cée?"

He reached across the book and turned another page, brushing his fingers against hers. After all these years, after all they'd been through, she was shocked that he could still send a thrill down her spine. Jess was right, she wasn't over him.

"Aw, come on. Zack and Ben are well-meaning enough, if a bit misguided."

She glanced at him. He was still wearing her father's hat. She knew she should have thought it childish, but she didn't. "What was that I heard as I went up the stairs, something about the GAG rules?"

"Nothing." He gave a wave.

"The three of you are adults now, you know. There is no GAG Club. Girls are allowed in the clubhouse."

"We were just goofing around." He stood. "You want me to carry some of these boxes down and we can go through them in the living room where there's more light?"

She looked up. "Don't you have work to do? I don't want to be a pest."

He offered his hand to help her up and she took it. As she rose to her feet, his fingers lingered against hers. Or was that just her imagination?

"I don't mind, really." He picked up the nearest box and stacked it atop another. "Besides, I'm in the thinking stage with this new project. I've got some sketches, but it's still gelling. I could use some busy work—helps me think."

"You don't mind? You're sure?"

"I was always honest with you, wasn't I, Abby?" The

box he held in his arms was all that separated them. From across the open flaps of the box she sensed that he wanted something from her. But what? Absolution? Forgiveness?

"Yes, you were always honest with me," she said softly.

"And we did have fun." He grinned.

She smiled. "We did have fun."

His gaze lingered over hers and then he looked away. "Just tell me which boxes, lady, and I'll haul 'em down."

The next morning Abby woke in the twin four-poster bed her parents had bought her when they'd moved to Land's End. Despite the howling wind and the rain that pounded on the windows all night long, she'd slept well.

She glanced at the clock beside the bed. It was almost seven-thirty. She slid out of bed and walked across the hall to the bathroom. Just as she was about to push in, Owen came out, startling her.

"Morning," he said cheerfully. Owen had always been a morning person. She was not.

"Morning." She glanced up sleepily to realize he was staring at what she was wearing. . . . Or what she was not wearing.

She had slept in just panties and a short strappy tee shirt. Obviously Owen had seen her in far less, but she felt strange just the same. Why was he looking at her like that? She hadn't checked the scales lately. Was she putting on weight at her hips?

She ducked under his arm and into the bathroom.

"Want tea?" he called after her as she closed the door in his face.

"Sure."

Finished in the bathroom, she peeked out the door to be certain Owen was gone before she slipped back to her room. She changed into shorts and a less-revealing tee before going downstairs. Edgar met her at the bottom of the steps.

"Hey, boy." She scratched under his chin and he chuffed with pleasure.

"I'm in here," Owen called from the living room.

She found him seated on the floor in front of the TV, watching the weather channel. He wore shorts and a tee shirt he'd gotten in a 5K Bay run. She had the same tee shirt packed in the car. They had run that one together.

"Storm's still moving this way." He held a mug of coffee in one hand. He pointed to the Doppler radar picture on the screen.

She knelt beside him, watching the image of the storm as it crept up the coast. "It's headed straight for us, isn't it?"

He sipped his coffee and nodded. "I imagine we'd better batten down the hatches. Secure anything loose in the yard. I think I'll go check on Mom and Dad next door, make sure they don't need anything and then see if Mr. and Mrs. Nester on the other side are prepared."

"Mr. and Mrs. Nester are still living? Wow. They must be a hundred years old."

He got up and switched off the TV. "He's ninety-four, she's only ninety-two."

Abby couldn't resist a smile as she followed Owen into the kitchen. "And still arguing?"

"Every cotton-picking day of the week. I was over there last week dusting her roses, and she was throwing his clothes out on the front porch." He lifted the kettle from the stove and poured boiling water into the teapot he'd already set out. "Said she was kicking him out. Something about him flirting with a redhead in the Big Mart."

She leaned against the counter, waiting for her tea to brew. "I always admired them. Can you imagine being together for that many years?"

"It would have to be the right person," he said.

She wondered if what he meant was that she had just been the wrong person. What she'd said was true—she did admire the Nesters. More accurately, she was jealous of them. She had hoped she and Owen would be together that long.

"Tea's up." He poured the hot brew into a cup for her and walked to the fridge, coming back with a wedge of lemon.

"Why are you being so nice to me?" she asked, still not entirely awake. She was never fully awake until her second cup of caffeine. "Running and fetching. Complimenting me. I expected to find my bed turned down with a mint on the pillow last night when I turned in."

He leaned against the counter beside her, resting one bare foot behind him on the cabinet, his elbows on the countertop. He was always so attractive in the morning with damp hair, and smelling like shaving cream. It had been mornings like this when they were married, back when things had been good, that they would start having breakfast and halfway through, end up in their bed making love. Sometimes they didn't make it to the bed.

She felt her cheeks grow warm and lifted the cup to her lips.

"What are you thinking?" he asked.

"None of your business. You didn't answer my question. Why are you being so nice?"

He walked away from the counter. "Because you deserve it. Because I was a shmuck."

"You weren't a shmuck."

He opened the refrigerator and peered inside. "I was a shmuck."

"OK." She laughed. "You were a shmuck."

"I put my career first instead of you," he said, taking eggs out. "Instead of us."

"Who was it who said that she had never heard a man ask how to balance his career and his marriage?" she mused, feeling entirely too melancholy for 7:30 in the morning.

"Exactly. Now, I'm not making excuses for myself, or anything." He set the eggs on the counter and retrieved a box of pancake mix. He avoided eye contact, but that was OK. She understood how hard it was for men to express feelings. It just wasn't in their DNA.

"But men aren't really taught to think about those things. Growing up, we get the idea that if we just bring home the bacon—"

"The little woman will serve as the caretaker to the house, the kids, the marriage."

He found a mixing bowl and grabbed a wooden spoon from a crock on the counter. "I know my parents certainly never talked about 'their relationship.' "

She sipped her tea. "Mine either."

"Anyway." He shrugged those hunky shoulders of his. "I'm sorry for the things I did, for things I didn't do, too."

They were both silent as he read the directions on the box and mixed up pancake batter. What could either of them say? They couldn't turn back the hands on the clock. So what if he was sorry? What was done was done. They were divorced. Their paths had split and they were headed in different directions. Right?

Abby wished Owen would say something else. He had said more to her since she arrived yesterday than he had through the divorce proceedings. He had been so docile about the whole thing, as if he'd been glad to get rid of her. Now she wondered if she had misinterpreted. Had he just been too stunned to know what to do? What to say?

The batter mixed up, he glanced at her. "I'm making pancakes," he said, as he plugged in an electric griddle. "Want some?"

She reached for the teapot to refresh her mug. "I shouldn't. I haven't run all week, but sure."

"Paper's on the table if you want it."

She wandered over to the kitchen table and leafed through the Land's End Daily, but she just skimmed the headlines. There was something in the room that made her edgy. Some kind of static electricity or something. It had to be from the storm. It made her feel as if her skin didn't fit right.

"Two medium-sized cakes coming up." He slid a plate in front her.

"Thanks." She glanced up. It felt so nice to be pampered like this. Having Owen do these little things for her made her want to do them for him, too. "I'm getting jam, you want that or syrup?" she asked, getting out of her chair.

"Jam will be fine. Should be some of Mom's strawberry preserves in there, I think."

She walked back to the table with the quilted Ball jar. "The wind sounds worse, if that's possible. You want me to go check on your mom and dad while you see the Nesters? If anyone needs anything from the grocery store we can combine efforts."

"You don't really want to do that. You stay here and write."

"I don't mind, really," she said, opening the jar and sliding it toward him. "I'd like to say hi to your mom and dad before I go anyway."

He made a face. "From the look of that radar screen you're not going anywhere today."

She glanced at the window. Rain was still falling. He was probably right. Even if the hurricane did pass at noon, the roads would be littered with debris. "You don't mind?"

"Mind? Of course not. Actually," he hooked his thumb, "I ordered this hurricane just so I could keep you in my lair, seduce you and make you mine again."

They both laughed, but something about the way he said it made her stomach give a little flip. Was Owen trying to say that he was still attracted to her? Was Jess right? Was he sniffing?

No, he was just being nice, being his old self.

"You go to the Nesters'," she said firmly. "I'll check on Mom and Dad." She had called the Thomases "Mom and Dad" for years, even before her parents passed away. "We'll meet back here and then run into town for anything anyone needs."

"Think we can beat the storm? We don't want to be out when that thing hits land."

She began to cut up her pancake. "It'll be an adventure."

"Sweetheart, every day of my life with you has been an adventure."

Abby was still smiling to herself when she went upstairs to dress.

Six

"Abby?" Owen's mother Lillian stood at the screen door and blinked. "Is that you, dear?" Her mouth, painted with pink lipstick, twitched.

Lillian looked as if she had just seen a ghost. Abby had obviously taken Owen's mother by surprise. Apparently, he had not told his mother she was passing through.

Abby angled her head downward to keep the driving rain off her face. She was wearing one of Owen's slickers over jeans, and a tee and sneakers. Everything was already wet that wasn't covered by the yellow slicker. "I just came by to see if you needed anything. Owen ran over to the Nesters'."

"Well," Lillian drew a breath. She had never quite lost her Georgia accent. "It certainly is a surprise to see you, dear."

Not necessarily a good surprise. Abby could tell by the older woman's tone.

"I . . . I'm on my way south. I stopped to get some things from my parents'—Owen's house," Abby corrected herself. "Then the storm." She gestured at the dark, turbulent sky.

"Oh, dear." Lillian's hands flew to her cheeks, and she backed up out of the doorway. "I'm so sorry. Where are my manners? Mama must be rollin' in her grave. Come in! I'm standin' here like a bumpkin while you're gettin' all wet." She spoke without *G*'s on the ends of her words. Owen claimed they'd been removed from her vocabulary at her first cotillion.

"Thank you," Abby murmured as she stepped into the mudroom off the kitchen. She had taken the back entrance because it was the door she and Owen had always used. Considering the way Lillian was acting, and now that she was no longer a part of the family, she wondered if she should have rung the front door bell.

"Maurice!" Lillian called into the kitchen. "Look what the hurricane has blown in. It's our dear Abby."

Abby felt warm and pushed back her hood. She stood, dripping on a rag rug she knew Lillian had sewn herself. "A lost art," Owen's mother had called it. Abby had one of Lillian Thomas's multicolored rag rugs packed in her car at this very moment. She had sold most of her possessions, put a few things in storage, but the rug would go with her because it reminded her of home. Every morning when she climbed out of bed in the little cottage on the sea she intended her bare feet to touch that part of home to keep herself grounded.

"Abby." Maurice, an older gray version of Owen appeared in the mudroom doorway. He threw open his arms and hugged her in a great bear hug.

"Dad," Abby laughed. "Don't. You'll get all wet." But she allowed him to embrace her and hugged him back.

"What the blast do I care?" He leaned back, grinning, his hands still resting on her shoulders. Maurice had always liked Abby and the two of them had always gotten along well. After Abby's father died, Maurice had served as a father figure throughout the remainder of her high school and college days. It was Maurice Thomas who had given her away on her wedding day.

"What the hell are you doing here?" Maurice bellowed.

Lillian moved to stand just behind her husband in the kitchen doorway. "Just passing through, weren't you, dear?"

"In a hurricane?" Maurice had always talked loudly, but since he had begun to lose some of his hearing, he was worse.

Abby couldn't stop smiling. It was so good to see him. "I didn't realize the storm had built into a hurricane when I left Boston," she explained. "Luckily, Owen was on top of things. I stayed over at the house last night."

Lillian's thin plucked eyebrows arched. "Did you?"

Abby's smile fell as she stumbled for an explanation. "Just until the hurricane passes, then I'll be headed south. I've rented a cottage. I'm writing a book."

"Won't you come in?" Maurice waved her into the kitchen. "Dry off, have a cup of tea?"

"I can't. I just wanted to see if you needed anything. Owen and I are going to run to the grocery store."

"We don't need a thing," Lillian said. "We've already run jugs of water and located candles, matches and such. Should there be a power shortage, we'll be ready."

If there was one thing Lillian Thomas always was, it was ready.

"Okay," Abby nodded, raising her hood again. "I just wanted to be sure. I already walked around the house, checked the locks on your shed doors, put your hose away."

"You didn't put the hose away?" Lillian turned on Maurice. "Do you know how dangerous a garden hose can be in a hurricane?"

Maurice ignored her as he had been ignoring her since their wedding day thirty-eight years ago. "We're glad you came by. If you're staying another night, come back over and pay us a visit. I want to hear all about that book of yours." He winked.

"Of course she's not staying over," Lillian injected with authority. "The hurricane will pass and she'll be getting on the road again, won't you, Abby?" she asked pointedly.

Abby pulled the hood of the yellow slicker down as far as she could to cover her face. "Well, we'll see. Owen thinks the roads may not be passable this afternoon."

"Stay a few days," Maurice encouraged. "We'd love to see more of you."

"Well, I'd better go. Owen wants to get to the store and get home. The hurricane was cutting inland last we saw on the radar." She smiled. "You two take care of yourselves. Call over to the house if you need anything."

Abby pushed through the back door and went back into the rain, chuckling to herself. It was true what people said—some things never changed. Lillian had never liked her, not since she and Owen were friends in the fifth grade. Owen always swore it wasn't personal. He said that in his mother's eyes, no one would ever be good enough for him. Oddly enough, Abby and Lillian had always gotten along. Abby just followed Maurice's example. She ignored her.

Abby cut across the lawn to Owen's, dodging flying bits of paper and whirling leaves. It was good to see Maurice, and even Lillian. More of home.

By noon the sky had darkened until it almost looked like night outside. The wind had taken a portentous groaning tone and the hurricane was headed up the bay. It wasn't a major hurricane, only a two on a scale of one to five, but just the same, it seemed ominous as it pressed toward the little town of Land's End on the eastern shore of the Chesapeake Bay.

"Coming right for us," Owen said grimly as he clicked off the TV and glanced over his shoulder. "Everyone in town seems well-prepared though. We should be fine."

Abby, who stood in the doorway, had been watching the weather station with him. She liked the way he said "we" should be fine, meaning Land's End. She missed being a part of that "we."

"They're not expecting much damage, then?"

"Nah."

She wasn't afraid of the hurricane, but it made her uneasy nonetheless. She didn't like the idea of something having such power over the lives of others. Hurricanes wrecked homes, families, and sometimes killed. She hugged herself, chilled. "I think I'll make tea."

"I can get it." Owen passed her, rubbing her arm as he went by. He knew storms made her uncomfortable.

She watched him make the tea. "Want me to make some cookies? Not as good as your mom's," he said over his shoulder. "Just scoop out, but I think they're pretty good."

She couldn't resist a smile. She was beginning to think he wasn't joking when he said he'd called up the storm in order to seduce her. Owen knew very well that the quickest way into her bed was a rainy afternoon with tea and chocolate chip cookies as foreplay. She knew her warning hackles should go up; Jess had told her this could happen. But she felt no need to back off or tell him to. Did that mean that secretly she wanted him to pursue her?

She didn't have the time or the money to spend the years it would take in therapy to discover the answer to that. . . .

"We could play Scrabble or something," Owen said.

"I was going to work," she said, not wanting to sound too enthusiastic, "but my battery isn't working right on my laptop and I don't suppose I ought to be plugging it into the wall right now."

"No way. I already disconnected mine. Could be power surges."

She smiled in surrender. "OK. Cookies and Scrabble it is." She didn't think she'd smiled this much in the last six weeks.

"You get the game and I'll throw the cookies in the oven. You know where it is."

"Front closet."

A short time later they were seated on the living room floor, tea and a plate of cookies beside them and a Scrabble board between them. Even with the lamps on, the room seemed shadowed. The wind screamed outside now, but inside, Abby felt safe, sheltered. And not just from the storm, but from the hardships of life. At this moment, it seemed as if there was no one in the world but her and Owen.

Surely, she wasn't falling for him again. Was she out of her mind?

Owen placed the word *set* on the board.

"A three-letter word?" she teased.

"I have a lot of Zs."

She laughed. "There are only two in the game."

She added a *T* and an *LE* to his *set* and wrote down her score. *"Settle?* What's a settle?"

"A couch. An eighteenth-century term."

"Ooooh." He made a sound as if he were impressed.

She threw one of her *T*'s at him.

Next he wrote *end* using the last *E* on her settle. He took a cookie and bit into it.

Abby found the aroma of chocolate mixed with his aftershave entirely too disconcerting. She tried to concentrate on the game. "Tell me about the new company," she said, trying to get her mind off Owen and the feelings running around inside her. Feelings she definitely didn't welcome.

"It was Zack's idea. After his divorce, he moved home. People were starting to discover Land's End, buying up houses, wanting to fix them up. Only there are no reputable companies nearby that know what they're doing when it comes to authentic restorations. You have to hire someone from Annapolis and bring equipment and stuff across the bay. That can get expensive."

"So, you're doing the design, Zack's doing the fine woodworking and Ben's hiring work out."

He stretched out on the rug on his side of the board, propping his head up with his hand. "That's the idea."

Owen was only 6′ 1″, but he seemed taller stretched out on the floor. She could see his biceps as he flexed them to hold up his head. He was still going to the gym. . . .

"And so far the response has been good?" She added an *ing* to his *end* for a double-word score and it was his turn again.

"It's been great."

She picked up new tiles. "It's really blowing out there now," she commented.

He glanced up, listening. "Should be right on us shortly." He added the word *kiss* using the *S* from *settle*.

Abby stretched out on her side so that she lay parallel to him with the board between them. How many games of Scrabble had they played over the years like this? She tried to concentrate on her available letters and beating him rather than on his blue eyes following her every move. He seemed to be breathing in time with her, making her entirely too aware of his body and her own. She wrote *doomed*. Was she?

Her hand was barely back from the board when he dropped his tiles into place. *You.*

He had written *Kiss you.*

She looked up at him, her gaze meeting his. His mouth was slightly upturned in a smile that told her he was unsure of himself.

"How did you manage that?" she asked softly, mesmerized by his eyes, by his mouth and the overwhelming need she felt to kiss him. She felt as if she was under a spell, or mind control or something. "Are you cheating?" she accused.

He shook his head, refusing to look away.

She swallowed. Red flags went up in her head. Caution!

Caution! She could almost hear Jess shouting, "Run away! Run away!"

But she couldn't.

"You asking?" she breathed.

"I think so." His words came out in a whisper. So genuine, so . . . vulnerable, if it was possible for a man to sound vulnerable.

Abby didn't say yes, but she didn't say no either. She felt frozen in time as he inched across the carpet toward her.

Owen's lips brushed hers and her eyes closed of their own accord. She could feel herself melting into the carpet. It had been so long since he had kissed her like that. A kiss she felt to the tips of her toes. And he was such a good kisser. . . .

They exchanged breath, their kiss tentative. Then Abby parted her lips slightly. She knew she was making a mistake. She was setting herself up for more heartache. This was not why she had come. But she couldn't help herself. Her body had a mind of its own.

Abby lifted her hand to his shoulder and she was on her back as he pressed her into the carpet, his tongue touching hers. He tasted of chocolate cookie and lost love.

The kiss deepened and his hand found her breast. The sound she had meant to make in protest came from her mouth as a sigh . . . nearly a groan.

Jess was right. Abby was desperate for sex and didn't realize it. So desperate she would go for it with her ex-husband.

"Abby, Abby," Owen whispered. "I've missed you so much."

Gone was the sound of the lamenting wind. Gone was the scratch of branches on the windows, the scrape of limbs against the siding and the squeak of shutter hinges. She heard nothing but Owen's voice and her own sighs of encouragement.

She made no protest when he slipped off her T-shirt and expertly unhooked her bra between her breasts. She watched as he peeled off his T-shirt and settled above her again. Her hand found the planes of his chest and she closed her eyes, flooded with memories. She had never made love with anyone but Owen. She couldn't imagine doing this, feeling this, with anyone but him.

Owen knew all the right buttons to push. He had always been a generous lover, even in their college days when they were bumbling through it. He covered her neck and her breasts with soft fleeting kisses. He teased her nipples into taut peaks with his tongue. He made her moan, made her groan. It felt so good.

Abby grazed her hands over Owen's bare back, over his shorts. She was past the point of protest. Her only thought now was of release. She'd deal with the penalty later.

Owen kissed his way up her neck, along her jawbone to her earlobe. "We don't have to do this," he breathed huskily. "Not if you don't want to." His tongue teased her lobe. "Not that I don't want to."

"No," she breathed, pressing her hips to his, feeling the familiar dampness in her panties. It had been so long. Too long. "I mean, yes, I want to."

"You're sure?"

She opened her eyes to meet his gaze and smiled. Maybe this was what she needed. One last time, just to get him out of her system. "I'm a big girl," she whispered. "A liberated woman. I can speak for myself." She lifted her head from the carpet and brushed her mouth against his. "And right now, I want you, Owen."

He slid out of his shorts and helped her out of her jeans. Last came the panties and they were naked on the carpeted floor, lying beside each other. Owen pushed the Scrabble board away with his bare foot. She heard the tiles scatter.

They kissed again and again. She couldn't get enough of the taste of him. It was as if she had been without water too long.

He traced the dip of her waist, her hip, her thigh, and then slid his hand inward. She parted her legs and rolled onto her back. She didn't have to give him directions, tell him what she wanted, what made her feel good. Owen knew instinctively . . . he knew.

When he finally lowered his body over hers and she parted her thighs to receive him, her heart was pounding, her veins pulsing with need. She could think of nothing but Owen and the desperate burning desire inside her to claim him as her own once more.

The union was better than she had remembered. They moved in unison, climbing higher, soaring until she cried out with pleasure. He followed behind her.

Satiated, Owen and Abby parted. She lay on her back on the carpet, in the crook of his arm. She kept her eyes squeezed shut as her body rippled with the last tremors of her orgasm.

"Wow," Owen muttered when he found his voice.

"Wow," she repeated. Then she turned her head and when she met his gaze, she burst into giggles.

He laughed with her and touched the end of her nose with his finger.

"I swear, that was not my intention when I sat down here," he told her.

She closed her eyes again, not yet willing to meet reality head-on. "Well, I can tell you it wasn't mine, either." She looked at him again. "But I'm not sorry."

He squeezed her shoulder. "We were really good together, Abby. We made such a good team. And I don't just mean in bed."

She tightened her lips together, afraid she might cry. She wasn't sure what he was trying to say or where he was trying to lead the conversation, but she knew she wasn't ready to go there. She stared at the ceiling. "Listen. It's quiet," she breathed.

He looked upward. "Eye of the storm."

She moved against him, feeling chilly all of a sudden, perhaps because it had been so damned hot in the room only a few moments ago. He reached behind to the couch and pulled off a cotton throw. He covered them both with it. "Better?" He kissed her temple.

She closed her eyes, refusing to cry. Refusing to think. She just wanted to lie here in his arms for a few minutes and enjoy the moment.

The next thing Abby knew she was waking up. The storm had passed and she was alone in the dark living room.

Seven

In the quiet darkness Abby reached for her clothes. She smiled to herself; Owen had folded them neatly and stacked them on the couch. The storm had passed and the house was peaceful once again. She slipped into her bra and pulled her T-shirt over her head.

She couldn't believe she had actually made love with him. Was she out of her mind? Was this the way she thought she was going to sever ties with him?

She pulled on her jeans and tucked her hair behind her ears. Where was he? She was caught between wanting to find him and wrap her arms around him, and wanting to sneak out the door and head straight for Myrtle Beach.

She crept out of the dark living room. "Owen?"

The front door was open and she spotted Edgar seated on the porch beside Owen. Owen was barefoot, dressed in just his T-shirt and shorts. When he heard her footsteps, he turned and smiled.

"Hey, sleepyhead."

His smile, meant only for her, made her warm all over.

She hesitated before stepping out onto the porch, uncertain of the protocol here. Was this like date sex? Were there rules? Or, because they had once been married, were they under the old codes? Did she slip her arm around him and lift on her toes to kiss him and smile like she used to? Did she make some comment about how wonderful their lovemaking had been? How good he had been? Or did she just wait to see what he would say?

He held out his hand for her and she went to him. She didn't put her arm around him because she felt awkward, but let him continue to hold her hand in his. It felt right.

"Hurricane passed," he mused.

She could tell by his tone that he was in one of his thoughtful moods. "I can see that."

The front lawn was strewn with branches and leaves and other debris. A shingle from someone else's house lay on the front brick walk. There was a garbage can in the middle of the street. Across the road, at the neighbors', she spotted a shutter that had pulled free and now rested on their porch roof. But all and all, the damage seemed minor.

Abby let out a sigh, relieved the loss wasn't worse. Relieved Owen seemed so relaxed with her. She would just follow his cue.

"Why didn't you wake me?" she asked, feeling shy and not understanding why. How could she feel shy? This was Owen, whom she had grown up with. Owen whom she had slept with, made love with for years. Now she felt silly.

He kissed the top of her head. He was smiling a gentle smile. "I don't know." He lifted one broad shoulder. "You looked so content. I didn't want to disturb you."

She stared at the painted gray floorboards of the Victorian wraparound porch, slipping her hand from his.

"Owen, I don't want you to think this . . . that that's why I came." She gestured lamely toward the house, the living room, and the scattered Scrabble board. "It . . . it was never my intention."

He caught her hand again; his face grew solemn. "You trying to say you wished we hadn't made love?"

"No. That's not what I'm saying." She searched his gaze. "I'm saying I didn't come here chasing after you or anything like that. Not like Ben and Zack probably think. It . . . it just happened."

He squeezed her hand. "I know that." He offered a hint of a boyish smile. "Though I was kind of hoping that was what you came for."

She laughed, pulled her hand from his and gave him a playful push. It felt good to laugh like this after they made love. That was what it was all about, wasn't it?

He glanced over the porch rail. "You know," he said. "There hasn't been anyone but you since the divorce. I went on a date or two, but it just wasn't right. Wasn't you," he said softly. "Never been anyone but you, Abby."

She swallowed. This was a dangerous path he was taking. She didn't want to hear anything that she could interpret to mean he wanted her back. Nothing that even gave a hint. It had been so hard for her to leave their marriage, a marriage that had not been good for either of them, not for a long time. It had been so heartbreaking. She couldn't open herself up to that pain again. She wasn't certain she could survive it without losing herself.

So, she needed to just come out and say so, didn't she?

She took a breath, gathering her thoughts. "Owen, you and I both know that divorcing was the right thing to do. You were miserable. I was miserable."

"Not because of you."

She ignored him. Why after all these years did he want to share his feelings now? Now when it was too late? "We were miserable with each other," she continued, following the script in her mind. "It didn't work. It just didn't work, and now we need to move on."

Her speech sounded good. She repeated all the things the women's magazines said a woman should say, but somehow none of it tasted right on her tongue. The words were bitter, sour, and something about them rang untrue.

He shook his head. His voice was gentle . . . drifting. "If I could go back, I would do things differently."

So would I, she thought, though she didn't say it. Jess said she needed to protect herself.

He turned to her. "How many ways can I tell you I'm sorry? That I screwed up? How many times would it take to make a difference?"

She ran her hand down the length of his arm, trying to ignore his last statement. He did want to fix it, but it couldn't be fixed, could it?

"You can't hold yourself entirely responsible," she reassured him. "I was in that house, too. I let you slip away from me."

Both of them were quiet for a moment. The wind had calmed, though the rain was still falling lightly on the porch roof overhead. Edgar sat on the edge of the porch and caught raindrops that slipped over the rail and down a corner post.

"Would you believe me if I told you I've changed?" Owen said. "That I'm not the same man I was when you left?"

She wasn't prepared for this. She tried to harden her heart. "Owen, please. It's too late."

"It's not too late!" He turned to face her. "It's not too late, Abby . . . not if we don't want it to be."

She walked back inside. Retreat! Retreat! her inner voice cried. Get angry. Anger will isolate you, rescue you, she told herself. Protect you. "This is crazy!" she shouted.

He followed. Edgar padded behind them.

"It's not crazy."

"Owen, these feelings you're having." She started up the stairs, afraid she was going to cry. "They'll pass."

"They won't pass. I never stopped loving you." He rested his hand on the finial at the bottom of the stairs and called up. "Did you hear what I said?" He shouted his last words. "I never stopped loving you!"

"Well, you sure as hell didn't act like it!" she threw over her shoulder.

Owen stood at the bottom of the staircase, feeling as if he'd just been drenched in cold water. He had no clever retort. No reply to fling back because she was right.

He listened to her footsteps die down the hall, followed by the distinct sound of a door slamming.

"Well, that certainly went well," he muttered under his breath.

Maybe he should let her go. Let her pack up and head to Myrtle Beach. He didn't need Abby. He didn't need a woman. It was like Zack and Ben and he had agreed over pizza and beer. They had each other.

He gave a dry laugh as he walked into his office followed by his faithful dog. Who was he kidding? Now that he was getting his life back together, now that his head was screwed on straight again, he was beginning to realize just how much he did need Abby.

So, he couldn't give up. He had to think of a way to keep her here until he could convince her that they could make their relationship work again. He had to make her fall in love with him again. She'd loved him once. Why couldn't she love him again?

The phone rang and Owen picked up the phone on his desk. He dropped into his chair. " 'Lo."

"Owen."

"Ben."

"Things OK at your place?"

Owen glanced up at the ceiling, thinking of the slammed door. "Just peachy."

"No damage?"

"Nah." Except maybe to his ego. "Maybe a loose shingle or two. And I think my wading pool blew away, so no pool party tonight, but other than that, the place is fine. How about you?"

"One broken window from a flying branch, but nothing else."

"Zack?"

"I already talked to him. He was going on about some herb bed, but as best I can figure, no damage there, either."

Owen picked up a mechanical pencil to doodle on his blotter. "How about anyone in town? Hear anything?"

"Power's out at the bowling alley. No phone service to Harbor Place." Harbor Place was a new housing development at the edge of town. "Other than that, nothing major."

Owen was sketching a diamond, filling it in, when he

spotted where Abby had written her name on his blotter. Looking closer, he saw where she had written Abby Thomas, then scribbled it out and written her maiden name instead. Ouch, that hurt. He wrote his own name below hers.

"So . . ." Ben said after a pause between them. "Must be weird with Abby in the house. What did you do all day?"

Owen caught a flash in his mind of Abby's bare breasts. He felt her lips on his. His groin tightened and he tried to think of cold showers and dental chairs. "Not much. Played some Scrabble. She took a nap."

Ben paused again. "So, she's on her way now?"

"Nah." He tried to sound casual. He didn't dare tell Ben the truth. That he wanted her to stay. That he had this notion he could make her love him again. Ben and Zack would be over here in no time with a straitjacket.

"She's going to stay until morning," Owen continued. "Power lines might be down. Stuff in the road. Besides, it's too late to head out now." He drew an ampersand between his and Abby's names on the blotter the way she had done on her notebooks back in high school.

"I see. Well, I think we're going to get together tonight. Penny poker. Want to come?"

He drew a big heart around their names. Curly queues. "I shouldn't leave Abby. That would be rude."

"She might be glad to get rid of you, buddy."

He grimaced. Ben probably didn't know how close he was to the truth right now. "I don't know . . ."

Ben made a sound into the phone, something akin to a groan of disgust . . . or disappointment. "So, bring her."

"Bring her?"

"Sure. Why not? Dad's invited some babe. We'll make it a party."

Owen grinned. Ben's mother had passed away a few years ago and for the last year, his dad, Max had been dating continually. It was a source of great amusement to the three of them. Max said he was looking for a good woman to share his life with and they were trying to get away from women.

"We'll play cards, get some pizza, have a few brewskies."

"Mint iced tea for Zack."

The two men laughed. Zack rarely drank beer and never anything with caffeine in it. He always said he lived on his own high.

"So, you're serious about bringing Abby?"

"Sure, why not? Bring the dog too if you want. Mom, Dad, anyone you can drag off the streets . . ."

Owen smiled. Ben was a good friend. "Sevenish?"

"Ish."

Owen hung up. An evening with the guys might be just what he and Abby needed to diffuse her anger with him. Maybe if he could get her relaxed again, she might be willing to talk.

Surprisingly enough, it didn't take much to convince Abby to go with him to Ben's for cards and pizza. Maybe she was over their argument earlier in the day, or maybe she just wanted to get out of his house. They pulled up to Ben's place just before seven.

"Wow," Abby said, sliding out of his Mazda sedan. "This is so neat."

Ben's house was a refurbished nineteenth-century brick and timber barn located on the back corner of a large property on the edge of town. The original manor house had burned years ago and a typical two-story colonial had been constructed in its place, but the barn still had its original character.

"Ben did this himself?" She stared up at the brick walls and cedar shake roof, her mouth open in awe. "It's beautiful."

"He hired it out. I drew up the plans; he found the men to do the work. Wait until you see the paneled wet bar and bookcases Zack built in the living room." He grabbed a six-pack of sodas from the back seat along with a bag of potato chips and a store-made onion dip. "It's incredible."

"You guys are amazing." She headed around the side, following the brick walk to the front door, still looking up at the brick wall that reached two-and-a-half stories into the dark sky.

Owen smiled to himself. She had said "you guys." That meant him, too, right? She thought he was amazing, too. So, that could be translated to mean she couldn't think he was too big a shmuck. Right?

He held open the door for her, wondering if he could figure out how to sabotage her car. If her car wasn't running, she couldn't leave Land's End.

Inside, everyone else was already there. Ben met them at the door and took Abby on a tour of the house, including the two upstairs loft bedrooms. Owen stayed downstairs.

Owen was tucking the sodas into the fridge when Max came around the corner into the kitchen with a woman on his arm. The seventyish woman was wearing a flowing purple caftan and she had red nails as long as daggers. Her skin was olive, her eye makeup heavy and metallic.

"Owen, did you meet my friend Delilah?" Max grinned.

Owen offered his hand. "Nice to meet you, Delilah."

She shook it and then adjusted her purple and green turban. Dyed blue-black tendrils peeked from the fabric. "Nice to meet you. I sense a good aura about you. Warm."

He smiled in lieu of anything one could reply to that.

Max always dated interesting women, but Owen couldn't help but wonder where he got this one from. A traveling fortune-teller's wagon?

"Delilah reads palms," Max explained.

Owen kept smiling. "Of course she does."

"I could read yours later, if you like, young man."

Over his dead body. Owen tucked his hands behind his back. "Well, thank you . . ." he muttered. "We'll . . . um . . . see how the poker goes." He glanced up, relieved to hear Abby's voice in the living room. "Better get this Coke to Abby," he said, grabbing one off the counter. Then he made his escape.

Owen and Abby were silent on the ride home from Ben's, but it wasn't a bad silence. More of a silence of reconciliation. She had enjoyed herself this evening. And she felt badly about shouting at Owen this afternoon, especially after he had made love to her. After he had said such nice things. But she was just so damned scared.

"I like Ben's house," she said finally, staring out at the familiar landscape they passed. Lawns were still littered with branches and leaves. Many houses were dark, but light still shone from some windows.

"It suits him."

"And it's so nice that he's figured out a way to have his dad there with him and both still have their privacy."

On the back of the barn a small efficiency apartment had been added, complete with a kitchenette. Max and Ben could come and go as they pleased, even with separate entrances, yet they were there for each other. Abby was impressed that Ben would be so considerate of his aging father.

"Ben's a good guy," Owen said.

She sighed and looked out the window again. She wanted to say she was sorry for this afternoon, but she didn't quite know how to broach the subject. And did she want to? She was leaving tomorrow. What would be the point? She ran her hand down her throat. It was feeling scratchy. She must have talked too much tonight.

"Owen," she finally said.

He looked at her. The dash light illuminated his face. "You don't have to say anything." His voice was soothing. "It's OK."

She smiled. It was so good to be with someone who knew her so well. "I guess I'll be going in the morning."

"You sure you don't want to stay one more day?"

There was something in his voice that made her tremble inside. He was asking her to stay. Worse, she wanted to stay. But she couldn't. She just couldn't.

"I really need to get going, Owen. I need to get started on my book."

There, she'd said it. She had no way out now. She had to go.

"I understand," he said quietly.

They were quiet for another half a block, and then he spoke again. He was making a concerted effort to sound cheery. "So, tell me about your book. Have it outlined?"

"Mmmhmm. Not chapter by chapter, just a synopsis, but I think I have a great idea."

"Can you tell me or is it, like, a top secret?" He waggled his eyebrows.

She laughed. "I can tell you. You might even have some good ideas. There's this one place where I'm not sure what should happen."

"Go ahead, I'm all ears."

They talked about her book the rest of the way home, then over tea and leftover cookies. It was after midnight when they finally parted at the top of the stairs, and as Abby said good night and closed her door behind her, she couldn't help wishing the hurricane had lasted just one more day.

Owen waited a good twenty minutes after Abby's light went out under her door before he crept down the hall, and down the stairs. Edgar followed in his footsteps.

Owen didn't want to let Abby leave tomorrow. He needed at least another day with her, another day for her to realize what a good guy he really was. To realize how much he still loved her.

Just one more day.

He made it to the front porch dressed only in his boxers before he realized that no matter how badly he wanted her to stay, he couldn't sabotage her car.

Reluctantly, he walked back into the house. He wanted

her to stay, but of her own choice . . . or at least due to a natural disaster.

Slowly, he climbed the stairs, dejected, trying not to be. Who knew? Maybe she would change her mind by morning. Maybe she would get up, come to his bedroom and say, "Owen. You're right. You have changed. You're a new man and I want to live the rest of my life with you. Slide over."

And maybe another hurricane would hit.

Eight

Abby woke to discover that overnight her scratchy throat had become raw and throbbing. She lifted her head off the pillow, then let it drop. She slid her hand over her forehead. Hot. Clammy. So, she had a fever, too.

Perfect.

She glanced at the bedside digital clock and bolted upright. Nine? It was nine in the morning already? That couldn't be possible, could it? She should have been on the road by now.

She forced herself out of bed and weaved her way down the hall. Maybe if she just got moving she would feel better. She didn't have time to be sick. She had to get out of here, out of Land's End, away from Owen before she did anything stupid. Anything she would surely regret later.

Abby brushed her teeth, but she could barely swallow. Twice she had to sit down on the toilet lid because she was dizzy with the fever. That was all she needed now—to fall and crack her head open in the bathroom and suffer a concussion. Writing a novel in a year was hard enough without mental disabilities.

She met Owen on her way back to her room. He had already showered, shaved and dressed. He smelled delicious and comforting, of shaving soap and fresh-brewed coffee.

The moment he saw her, his face lined with concern. "Abby, what's wrong?"

"I don't know," she croaked, passing him on her way back to her room. "My throat is really sore." She lowered herself to the edge of the bed. She was wearing nothing but panties and a T-shirt but what did that matter? He had seen her yesterday stark naked on the living room floor.

He sat beside her on her rumpled bed and pushed her hair out of her eyes. His cool fingers brushed her forehead. He was giving an awfully good impression of someone who cared about her. That's what ex-husbands did though, hit you with comfort when you were vulnerable, she tried to remind herself. He smoothed her hot brow. "You're burning up, sweetie."

She fell backward onto the bed, bare legs still dangling over the side. "No kidding." She couldn't believe her lousy luck. And she thought she was going to make a clean escape at seven this morning.

She shaded her eyes from the sun that seemed to pulse through her window. "Say, you didn't poison me with that onion dip last night, did you?"

"Poison you?"

"Just mild poisoning. A touch of arsenic or hemlock," she said. "To keep me in your lair."

He laughed. "It wasn't the dip, silly. The chocolate chip cookies—only yours, of course."

"Of course." She let her arm fall and closed her eyes.

The brightness of the sun and his handsome face were just too much for her.

He rested his hand on her bare thigh, rubbing it back and forth. It felt good, not in a sexual way, but in a comforting way. He honestly was worried about her. "You need to see a doctor right away."

"Maybe it will pass," she groaned. But already she could feel her throat constricting. She had a feeling she had strep. She had always been susceptible to the germ.

"Come on, get dressed." He got up and began to sort through her overnight bag, removing a clean shirt, shorts, panties and a bra.

She sat up and snatched her panties out of his hand. Powder blue. She'd bought them at a lingerie shop, not a department store. Just to make herself feel good. Certainly not for him. "Get dressed? I can't drive to Myrtle Beach like this."

"Not to Myrtle Beach, goose." He sat beside her again. "To the hospital."

She frowned, staring at him. She wasn't thinking clearly. Her temperature had to be over a hundred. "The hospital?"

"You're not waiting for an afternoon appointment with a doctor. You can run into the ER, get a prescription for an antibiotic and be out of there in no time. You know it's got to be strep. You've had it before."

"I don't want to go to the ER," she moaned. But even as she protested she reached for the clothes on his lap.

"Want help?" he asked.

"You wish." She got to her feet. "Out."

"Just with your undies?" he teased. "I love lacy undies."

She would have thrown her sneaker at him if she'd had the energy to reach down and pick it up. "Get out and make me some tea. I'll be down in a minute."

He hung on the doorjamb. Why was he smiling? She was sick and he was smiling?

"Looks like you'll be staying another day or two," he said with a smirk.

She was able to reach the sneaker, but missed the running target.

"So, what did he say?" Owen walked beside her, out of the automatic doors of the emergency room's lobby.

"She," Abby corrected.

"She?" He unlocked the car door for her and went around to the driver's side.

"Mm-hm." Abby slipped in and fastened her seatbelt. She rested her head on the backrest. "Dr. Kayla Burns, she's new in town."

"And?" He inserted the key in the ignition and started the car.

"Test was positive, right off the scale. Strep." She closed her eyes. "Maybe, if I'm lucky, I caught it soon enough to prevent the rash."

"What rash?" He pulled out of the parking lot and onto the street.

She glanced at him. "Don't you remember that icky rash I had right after we were married? I came down with strep and the rash followed." She closed her eyes again.

"Is it serious?"

"Nah, not as long I have an antibiotic. If I do get the

rash it will be itchy and look gross for a few days but no permanent damage."

"Do we need to find a drugstore?" He punched on the air conditioner. It was going to be another hot sticky day.

She shook her head and tapped her purse. "Dr. Burns wrote me out a script to get filled right in the pharmacy at the hospital. I took the first dose at the water fountain."

"Need anything else? Soda? Chicken noodle soup?"

She leaned against the window, her eyes still closed. "No, thanks. Just sleep."

"Well, I'll get you right home. I'm supposed to meet my team for my first practice at noon, but I can stay home with you if you want me to."

She opened her eyes. "You got a team?"

"I called while you were inside. The league had one team without a coach—the boys are all mine," he said proudly.

She reached out and patted his hand. "You go play ball with your team. I'll be fine. And when you come home you can tell me all about it. By then I ought to be coherent again.

This time it was Owen who reached across the seat to touch her. "I'm really sorry you're sick," he said, rubbing her arm.

She exhaled. "I feel bad about being an imposition like this, but the doctor said no travel for at least three days. I'm contagious." She laughed and then choked it back because it hurt too much. "I just hope you don't get it." The thought of his mouth on hers yesterday flashed through her mind.

"I won't. You know me, I never get sick. Anyway, I

said I was sorry you were sick. Not sorry that you're stay-ing."

She exhaled. Maybe it was the fever, but Owen could be so convincing when he wanted to be. So damned ap-pealing. "Let's not talk about this now."

"Later?" he asked. "Because I meant what I said yes-terday. About having changed."

"Maybe tomorrow when I feel better. OK, Owen?"

She could tell he was smiling by the way he spoke, though her eyes were closed. "OK, Abby."

Owen tucked Abby into bed, left a glass of ice water beside her and Edgar at the door to stand guard. "Anything else you need?" he asked from the doorway.

She had rolled onto her side, her head cradled in her hands, her eyes shut. He had always loved to watch her sleep like that.

"Nah," she mumbled. "Go play ball."

He wanted to go back to the bed and kiss her, but he thought that might be too pushy. He left the door open a crack so Edgar could get out if he wanted, then headed downstairs.

He really was sorry Abby was sick. But he couldn't help seeing this as a good omen. Maybe God thought she belonged here with him, too.

Whistling to himself, he grabbed his baseball glove and his clipboard with drills already outlined on sheets of pa-per, and jumped into his car. Practice and games were held at the same public ball fields he had played at as a boy. Ben and Zack were already there by the time he ar-rived.

"Hey, buddy," Ben called as he unloaded equipment from the back of Max's old pickup. Max would be coaching with his son.

Owen waved. There were little boys milling around Max's truck, helping Ben unload the bats and balls and other equipment, calling him "coach." Owen couldn't wait to meet his own team.

Zack was parked beside Ben, unloading equipment from his ancient landcruiser. His daughter Savannah had a batting helmet on and was taking practice swings.

"You guys practicing here?" Owen asked, squinting in the bright sunlight at the baseball diamond surrounded by chain-link fence. There were four fields in the complex and a fifth being built.

"We're going to run a few drills, then scrimmage," answered Ben.

Owen nodded. "Well, give me a few days with my boys and maybe we'll scrimmage with you."

"Sure. We'll check our schedules."

"I'm going to run over to the concession stand, meet with the director and then have a look at my team. You guys have a good practice." Owen put up his hand.

Ben and Zack waved back.

At the closed concession stand, Owen found Amy Loren, the league's director, sorting through uniforms in a storage room. He knew her from high school.

"Hey, Amy."

She didn't get up. "Hey, Owen. I'm so glad you called."

"Me, too." He adjusted his Orioles baseball cap, wondering what team he was actually getting. Ben had the Marlins, Zack, the Pirates. In Land's End teams had real baseball names. They weren't "Joe's Garage" or "Betty's

Grill," Amy had explained over the phone. She said the citizens of Land's End didn't want to make their kids "walking billboards." Instead, the league paid for its uniforms and equipment with donations and fund-raisers, and relied heavily on volunteers.

Amy got up from a pile of uniforms. "We were afraid we were going to have to disband the team. The first manager we had was transferred, effective immediately. I was desperate."

"I'm just glad I could help. Now that I'm back in town, I'd really like to be a part of the community."

"Well, let me take you down to your team. They're already there, waiting to start practice."

"Great."

Owen followed Amy past the field Ben and Zack were using. He waved to several men he knew from high school. Now they were dads themselves and coaching their sons' teams.

Amy led him to a baseball diamond, only Owen immediately realized it was a softball field. There was no pitching mound. Baseball was played with a mound, softball without.

He rubbed the back of his neck nervously as she led him around the field to the sunken dugout. He could hear voices. A squeal of laughter, most definitely feminine. These were girls. Girls? He wasn't coaching a girls' team. He was coaching boys. Maybe Amy was just stopping by another field on her way to the field where his boys would play.

"Coach Thomas, meet your team. The Red Sox." She gestured to a row of eight-year-old girls, all wearing red ball caps. "Ladies, this is your new coach, Coach Thomas."

Owen stared at the girls for a moment in utter confusion. Pigtails, hair scrunchies, purple bike shorts. Obviously there was a mistake. He didn't know anything about little girls. He'd never been one. He lowered his voice. "Um, Amy, I think there's been a little mistake here. I volunteered to coach a boys' team. Baseball, you know, hardball, five ounces, nine inches in circumference, 112 stitches." He pointed to a ball lying on the ground at his feet. "That's definitely a softball," he said quietly. "And those are girls."

She stared at him. There it was again, the 'you're-a-shmuck' look. Could all women make a man feel like a shmuck just by looking at him?

"You don't want to coach the team?" She did not lower her voice.

Little heads snapped in their direction.

He turned his head, his words meant only for Amy. A little redhead with a "Girls Kick Butt" T-shirt was staring at him, thrusting her fist into her glove.

"I wanted to coach a boys' team," he whispered under his breath. "I know baseball. I know boys."

"Owen, we don't have a boys' team available." She pointed at the girls waiting patiently on the bench. "We have the Sox and they need a coach. The season starts next week."

He looked away and accidentally caught the eye of the little redhead. She was directing the shmuck look at him, too. Obviously, females learned young.

"I don't know anything about softball." It came out very close to a plea.

"Here's the league's rule book. Pee Wee Softball." She thrust it into his hand. "Same as Pee Wee Baseball, only no sliding, no stealing and one base on an overthrow. Any questions?" She was already walking away.

Owen clutched the rule book and stared at the twelve little girls lined up on the bench. Sure, he had a million, but where to start?

"I don't know much about girls," he hollered after Amy.

"Same as boys," she called back.

He could have sworn he saw her laughing as she cut across another field.

Owen turned to the bench of eight-year-olds. All of them had gloves on their hands, red ball caps on their heads. They were staring him with big brown, blue and green eyes. They all had the shmuck look on their face.

The redhead spoke up. She had on a pair of shin guards. Catcher and captain of the team, of course. "So, Coach." She chewed on a hunk of pink bubble gum the size of a walnut. "You want to get us started with practice, or you want me to?" She didn't blink.

Owen swallowed hard, as frightened as he had ever been in his life. How could he coach a team of little gum-popping girls in pigtails?

And what was he going to tell the guys?

Nine

"Girls?" Abby sat up in bed and clapped her hands, laughing. "You're kidding?"

Owen stood sheepishly in her bedroom doorway. "I wish I was." He looked as if he'd been wrung through one of those old ringer washing machines.

She scooted over in bed and patted the mattress. She was feeling a little better. The antibiotic and ibuprofen had to be kicking in. Between the medicine and the three-hour nap, she was nearly feeling human. "So, how did it go?"

He sat on the edge. "About as badly as you could expect." He threw up his hands. "I don't know anything about little girls."

His words struck a cord in Abby. One of her final reasons for leaving Owen had been that she wanted children and he didn't. They had always discussed having a family. Owen always said he wanted children if she did, but when it came to it, he had never been ready. All he ever spoke of was his career and "getting settled" before they started their family. After a while she had begun to wonder if he didn't want children at all. She had finally given up bringing up the subject—one more crumbled brick in the foundation of their marriage.

"Oh, and you do know about little boys?" she questioned with a raised eyebrow.

"I know a thing or two." He traced a geometric pattern on the sheet that covered her. "I was a boy once. I know how boys think." He shook his head. "When they say women come from Venus and men from Mars, they're not kidding."

She drew up her knees, smiling. It was good to see Owen uncomfortable with a situation. He had been such a perfectionist in the past that he never attempted anything he feared he might not succeed at from the beginning. This was something new for Owen. Could this be evidence that he really had changed?

"So, what did you do with your team, *Coach?*"

"We hit for a while. I thought that would be good because I figured everyone likes to hit, even girls."

She nodded. "OK, so that went well?"

"It went fine after the ten minutes it took the girls to get their ponytails straight in their batting helmets," he said with exasperation.

She covered her mouth to keep from laughing outright at him. "What else did you do?"

"Then I tried to run a catching and throwing drill, but someone fell and scraped her knee and it took all twelve of them to get a Band-Aid and clean her up."

Abby covered her smile with her hand.

"Then we practiced base running and I wanted to time the girls from home to first but they voted and vetoed that idea. They all agreed they didn't want to run for times for fear of making someone else feel inadequate. Then someone got hit in the ear with a ball and started to cry. After that everything pretty much fell apart. I fell apart."

"There's nothing wrong with crying when you're hurt," Abby defended.

He gazed at her sternly. "Boys don't cry."

"Boys don't cry because men are not comfortable dealing with the emotions that go with tears," she explained. "We teach boys not to cry and tell girls it's OK. It's even expected. You took a psych class or two in college, you know that's not healthy."

He put his head in his hands. "I just don't know if I can do this, Abby."

"Are they badly behaved? Are their skills that poor?"

"No," he said slowly. "They're nice enough little girls. Very polite and considerate of each other. Far more considerate than boys. And their skills are actually very good. They're just . . . so *different.*" He lifted his hands, his palms facing heavenward. "They're girls," he said, as if that explained everything.

Abby lay back on the pillow again. "You're not going to quit, are you?"

He grimaced. "I can't. They like me," he complained. "They're calling me 'Coach' and I have to pick up the outfits Wednesday before practice."

"The outfits?" Her mouth twitched, but she suppressed her smile this time.

"Uniforms," he exhaled. "Only they call them 'outfits' and by the end of the hour-and-a-half practice, they had me calling them 'outfits,' too."

She crossed her arms over her chest and studied him. After a moment of silence, he glanced up.

"What?"

She laid her hand over his on the mattress. "I'm just proud of you," she said. "I know this is hard for you."

"It's just that they're really nice girls and there isn't anyone else," he said, as if needing to justify himself. "The director said that if I didn't take the team, it would have to be disbanded. The girls couldn't play the season."

"I think you're doing the right thing. A good thing. You might even have more fun than if you'd taken a boys' team."

"The guys are really going to give me a hard time about this," he said.

"Yup. They are. But you can handle them. Besides, wait until you tell them I'm here for a few more days. Then they'll have something better to give you a hard time about."

"I don't care what they have to say about you," he said firmly. "I want you here." He turned and placed one hand on each side of her waist and leaned over her. "In my love lair . . ."

She giggled as if they were college students again, sneaking into each other's dorm rooms.

"Want anything?" he asked.

He didn't move away and she didn't mind. She liked looking into his eyes. "No, thanks. I've got my book." She patted a hardback on the bed beside her. "I think I'll just read."

"OK." He tucked the sheets around her. "I'm going to go downstairs and work for a while. I've had an idea rolling around in my head all day. You just holler if you need me." The mattress shifted as he got up from the bed.

She picked up her book and pressed it to her chest.

Then he surprised her by leaning over to kiss her. "You'll get my germs," she warned, but she didn't pull away.

He brushed his lips against hers in a husbandly kiss that reminded her of old times. "Germs don't scare me. Nothin' scares me." His gaze met hers. "Except maybe you."

She was still smiling when he left the room.

Owen had been working on a preliminary sketch of the McClusky house for more than an hour when he heard the familiar rumbling of a small engine coming up the driveway. With a grin, he went out the front door. Edgar followed with interest.

Max rode up the driveway in his lawn tractor. The older man waved and Owen waved back. Since Ben's father had given up his license the previous year, his lawn mower had been his independent mode of transportation. When Ben first returned to Land's End, he had protested. He worked from an office in his home, so he argued that he could take his father anywhere he wanted to go. Or his father could always call the senior bus. Ben didn't like the idea of his father driving all over town on a lawn mower. People would think Max was kooky.

But Max refused to give in. He liked the idea of coming and going as he pleased. It had worked fine before Ben came to town. He didn't like having to depend on other people, or on a bus schedule. He liked his "John Deere" and the independence it provided and Max had declared that if Ben didn't like it, he could go soak his head.

Max pulled up to the sidewalk and cut off the engine.

From a bicycle basket attached to the back of the lawn mower, he removed a cardboard tube used to transport architectural blue prints. "Delivery for Mr. Owen Thomas," he said cheerfully.

Spotting who it was, Edgar began to pace the porch, chuffing excitedly. The dog loved Max.

"Want to come in for some iced tea?"

Max came up the steps. He was wearing shorts and a plaid shirt and a red ball cap on his bald head that said "Over the Hill and Still Sassy." "You got time? I don't want to be a bother."

"No bother. I've been working, but I was ready for a break." He held the door open for Ben's dad.

Max fished a doggie treat from his shirt pocket and slipped it to Edgar as he went into the house. The dog snatched the treat and bolted for the kitchen. He always ate his treats by his bowls.

"Saw you with your team," Max said with a chuckle as he followed Owen into the kitchen.

"Oh, yeah?" Owen found two glasses and poured iced tea for them both. He'd take some up to Abby later, when she woke.

"What happened? Ben said you had another boys' team. Said his team was going to whip yours."

Owen lifted his shoulders in a shrug. "The softball team needed a manager and I agreed to take it. It's all the same at this age."

"Well, you just keep telling yourself that, son." Max waggled a finger. "And don't let those boys razz you too much about having a girls' team. I think it's a good thing you're doin' there."

"Want lemon?" Owen crossed to the refrigerator.

"No, thanks. Just lots of sugar and none of that artificial stuff either. Kills rats in labs, you know—if they eat 2.5 pounds a day for a year-and-a-half." He sniggered at his own joke. "Got to be true. Read it in one of those health magazines."

"Two iced teas coming up." Owen sliced lemon for himself. "We can sit on the front porch in the rockers if you want. It's not too hot out."

"Suits me."

Max's attitude was contagious. He was always such a happy man, not like so many senior citizens Owen encountered in grocery stores, at the post office, or in line at the bank. Max never acted as if anyone owed him anything, and he enjoyed every moment of the day—every ray of sunlight, every drop of dew on the grass, every smile from people he passed on his lawn mower. Owen wanted to grow up to be just like him.

Max leaned against the counter, waiting for Owen to finish with the tea. "You see in the paper where they got a new manager for the sewer plant?" he asked, making conversation. "I sure hope—"

The sound of footsteps in the hall made Max and Owen both glance through the doorway.

It was Abby, barefoot and wearing nothing but one of Owen's T-shirts and probably a pair of panties hidden beneath the hem. Her hair was a mess, her cheeks red with her fever, and she was the most beautiful sight Owen thought he'd ever seen.

"Well, there," Max said, glancing at Owen, then back at Abby.

Abby halted in the hallway. "I'm sorry. I didn't . . . I didn't know you were here, Max." She gestured lamely to Owen. "Didn't know you had company." She turned on the balls of her feet, obviously embarrassed.

"What do you need, hon?" Owen put down the spoon he'd been using to stir Max's tea and went into the hall.

She was already halfway up the stairs. He could see a shimmer of the pale blue fabric of her panties as she hurried upward.

God, he loved this woman. He loved the way the muscles of her legs flexed as she climbed the stairs. He loved the way the hem of his tee shirt swung back and forth across her shapely rear end.

"Abby?"

"It's okay. I just wanted some hot tea, not to give a show." She self-consciously ran her hand over the rear hem of the T-shirt as she turned the corner at the top of the stairs.

Owen almost bumped into Max in the front hall.

"On the porch?" the older man asked, holding up the two glasses of iced tea.

Owen bobbed his head and held open the door. "Sure, just let me run a cup of tea up to Abby."

He went to the kitchen and fixed Abby's tea, leaving it in her room because she was in the bathroom. He knocked on the door. "Tea's in your room. Need anything else?"

"No, thanks," she said in a small voice.

Owen went downstairs and out on the porch. "Abby . . . she, she's not feeling well. Actually, she's pretty sick," he explained to Ben's father.

"You don't need to give this old man an explanation." Max passed him his iced tea from his seat in one of the old painted rockers on the front porch. "Not my business what you do. Not Ben's or Zack's business neither."

Owen sat down and sipped his tea. "She was supposed to go on to Myrtle Beach, but she's too sick. She'll probably be here several more days."

"Perfect opportunity." Max slurped his iced tea.

Owen's head snapped. "What did you say?"

"I said 'perfect opportunity.' " He peered at Owen over the wire rims of his eyeglasses. "You need a hearing aid, son?"

"A perfect opportunity for what?"

"To get her back, of course." He slurped again, obviously liking the home-brewed tea.

"Get her back?"

"I'm not stupid. I saw the way you looked at her at my place last night. Saw the way she looked at you when you was lookin' the other way." He shook his head. "Can't miss true love. And let me tell you something, son." He waggled that finger he was so fond of waggling. "It doesn't come often enough in a lifetime to turn it away."

"Max, you know the story." Owen glanced at his feet. "Abby left me. We're divorced. She's moving to Myrtle Beach to write a best-selling novel."

"She's not gone yet." Slurp.

Owen raised his head, smiling. Leave it to Max to lift his spirits. "You saw her looking at me?"

"Moonin' would be a better description."

Owen gave a little laugh. "I've certainly seen no evidence of mooning. I got the distinct feeling she just wanted to get away from me."

"What do you expect?" Max demanded. "You acted like a jerk. Practically invited her to divorce your butt."

Owen chuckled. "You're right. You're always right Max."

"Took me a lot of years to be right once in a while."

For a moment, the two men just sat in their chairs, rocking, drinking their tea, one sipping, the other slurping.

"You really think I have a chance?" Owen asked finally not daring to take his gaze off the rhododendron bush in the front yard.

"A chance for sure."

"Zack and Ben think I should send her off with good riddance."

"Don't take this the wrong way, but sometimes Zack and Bennett got mouse droppings for brains. They jus haven't met the right woman. Don't know what it is to really love and be loved. Love so hard it hurts." Max rocked rhythmically. "Personally, I thought the three o you were cracked, making that pact. Swearing of women!" He gave a snort of disgust. "Women are the best gift God gave men, far as I see. That's why I'm looking for another myself. My wife and I, we really loved each other and I miss her. Want that again."

Owen set down his tea, not thirsty anymore. "So, wha do you think I ought to do?"

"Keep her here. Show her you love her." His gray-green eyes were peering from the folds of suntanned skin "Show her you can be the man she needs you to be."

"I'm just not sure how long I can keep her here."

"You can't do any more than try your best." Max rose "Well, gotta roll. Places to go, women to see."

Owen accepted the empty glass Max pushed into his hand. "Thanks for coming by. I appreciate the delivery and the words of wisdom."

"Good luck," Max called, waving over his shoulder.

Owen watched with amusement as Max climbed on board his lawn mower, backed out of the driveway and headed back down the street.

Max said he had a chance. He thought Abby still loved him. He couldn't stop smiling.

The next morning Owen woke to hear Abby's voice coming from the bathroom. "Oh, no," she moaned.

He slid out of bed and went to the closed bedroom door that opened directly into the bathroom. He tapped on the door sleepily. "Abby, you all right?"

"Yes," she said, sounding defeated.

"What's wrong?"

"The rash." He heard footsteps and her voice from just the other side of the door. "It's all over me, Owen."

He pressed his hand on the paneled door. He could almost feel her warmth through it. "That's too bad. There's some hydrocortisone cream in the cabinet. That will help the itch."

"It will be days before this goes away," she moaned, still just inches away from him on the other side of the door.

"Abby."

"Hmm?"

"I'm glad you'll be staying a few more days."

Ten

"Place your hands against the wall, and no one gets hurt."

Owen was in the side yard, between two lilac bushes, cleaning up the aftermath of the storm when he heard Zack's voice. He straightened up, bringing the hamburger carton and the soda can with him. "What are you doing?" he asked as he turned around.

Zack was standing in the shrubs directly behind him, wearing a red bandana tied around his face like a bank robber. Ben stood beside him, wearing a paper napkin tied in the same fashion. Apparently they'd been to the donut shop this morning.

"You heard me, Mister," Zack ordered and gave him a playful shove. "Turn around and put your hands up."

Laughing, Owen dropped the trash as his buddies spun him around and threw him against the house, TV cop style. Ben started frisking him.

"What are you looking for?" Owen asked, still laughing. "Come on, guys. Someone is going to see you and call the police."

"We have reports, sir, that you have a woman hidden on your person," Zack said in a pseudo-official voice.

"A woman? On my person?"

His search complete, Ben slapped him on the back. "OK, you can turn around, but no sudden moves."

Owen wondered if any of his neighbors were watching. If Mrs. Grayson across the street spotted them, she would have the media alerted within minutes. He turned to face Zack and Ben. "What are you two babbling about? Did you skip your medication again?"

"OK," Ben conceded. "Actually, it's our understanding that you have a woman on the premises, not your person." He pointed to the wall. "I've just always wanted to try that."

Owen reached out and yanked the paper napkin off Ben's face. "Go away. Go home. Go back to the psycho ward; your weekend pass has expired."

"She was supposed to leave," Zack said, pulling his bandana down around his neck.

Owen grabbed up the trash again and pushed his way through the lilacs. "I suppose Max told you she was here."

"Dad knew?" Ben glanced at Zack. "Dad knew and didn't tell me?" He looked back at Owen. "Dad didn't say a word. We saw the car parked around back. Sly move, hiding her car, buddy, but not sly enough for us."

Owen picked up another tin can that had rolled into his yard during the hurricane. He was quickly moving from amused to annoyed. He knew his friends were honestly trying to look after him, but he wasn't sure he appreciated it. They obviously didn't understand what Abby meant to him. They didn't realize how much he loved her. "I didn't *hide* her car. I moved it. And since when are the two of you spying on me? Next thing you know, you'll be using ladders to peep in my bedroom windows."

"We just don't want to see you hurt, you know that, man." Zack picked up a fallen branch and followed Owen around to the dumpster near the back porch.

"She's sick." Owen opened the lid, tossed the trash in and reached for the branch Zack held.

"You really should have a compost heap."

Owen jerked the branch out of Zack's hand, threw it into the dumpster and slammed the lid. "She has strep throat. She saw the doctor and her orders were no traveling."

"Honest?" Ben leaned on the porch rail and crossed his arms over his chest.

"Honest."

Ben glanced up at the windows on the second story. "So, she's here a few days, gets better, and is on her way. No hanky panky."

Owen wondered whether he ought to just come right out and tell Zack and Ben that he was hoping he could convince Abby to stay, that he wanted to have another go at the relationship. But he didn't have the energy or the inclination to argue with them about it. They would just make it more difficult for him. Once he and Abby had things straightened out, he would tell them and they would have no say in the matter. But if he told them now, they'd be here day and night, trying to sabotage his plans.

For the first time in their long relationship, Owen felt ages older than his friends.

"No hanky panky," Owen repeated as he glanced at

Ben and grimaced. "Hanky panky? Nice choice of words."

Ben shrugged. "Dad. You can take the man out of the 1940s, but you can't take the '40s out of the man."

"So, you're OK, buddy?" Zack untied his bandanna and stuffed it into his pocket. "You don't need the ex-wife exterminators or anything? Because we've got that costume in the van, too." He hooked his thumb. "A cross between Ghostbusters and the Terminator."

Owen laughed. "You guys are nuts. Now get out of here. Don't you have a job or something?"

He headed around the front of the house, hoping he could lead them to their car. Abby was napping now, but she had said she would come down and sit on the front porch when she got up. She was starting to get claustrophobic in the house. He had made fresh lemonade for her.

"Hey, by the way, speaking of girls' softball teams, what's up?" Ben asked as they reached Zack's old VW microbus.

And Owen had thought he was almost in the clear. "No one said anything about softball." He jerked open the driver's door. "Have a nice day. Please don't come again."

"We saw you over at the softball field." Zack made no move to get into his van. "What happened? Your team not show up?"

Owen let out a moan. "That is my team."

"What?"

"The Red Sox. They're my team."

"You're coaching girls?" Ben exclaimed.

"You, go, girl!" Zack punched Owen playfully in the arm.

"Look." Owen glanced away, then back at his friends. "They needed me to coach a girls' team so that's what I'm going to do. And I don't want to hear any of your garbage, so just get out of here. Both of you."

"Girls?" Ben taunted, walking around to the passenger's side of the van.

"That's right, girls. Girls who could beat your boys," he snapped back.

Owen didn't know where that came from. He wished he could suck it back in, as quickly as he had let it out.

"Is that right?" Ben said slyly. "You want to play us?"

Owen pointed. "We want to beat you."

"Can you believe what he's saying?" Ben hollered to Zack over the roof of the jeep.

Zack threw up both hands meaning he was staying out of it. "Hey, Savannah is on my boys' team and she hits farther than any of them. I'm not siccing any girls on my poor little team."

Owen flashed a grin at Ben. "Want to take it back? Save a little face, buddy, while you still have the chance?" Owen was, of course, all bark and absolutely no bite.

"You kidding?" Ben swung into the jeep. "Give us a week or two and once the season starts and we have an official schedule, we'll set it up."

"You're on." Owen pointed and then let his hand drop as Zack backed out of the driveway.

His team of bubble gum-popping, pigtailed girls against Ben's team? Was he out of his mind?

"You challenged Ben's team?" Abby laughed, drawing her feet up under her.

She was wearing another one of his T-shirts and a pair of old sweatpants. Her hair was messy, her skin splotchy with the rash, but to Owen, she was beautiful in the fading afternoon light.

They were sharing a pitcher of lemonade on the front porch. The air was warm and humid, but the oppressive heat so prevalent in August on the Chesapeake had not yet returned. The cicadas were chirping in the trees, and Owen could hear the faint hum of a lawn mower somewhere down the street.

In his fantasies, this would be his life: a job he loved, this porch, the smell of freshly cut grass and Abby as his wife again. He could picture it in his mind's eye—Abby laughing, brushing her hand against his. Abby making promises for later in the evening when they would retire to the king-sized bed they shared.

"And Ben is serious?" she asked, tearing him away from his little fantasy.

"He's serious."

She lifted her eyebrows. "And you're going to do it?"

"I said I would. I guess I have to," he said, backing down a little.

"Come on." She punched his arm lightly. "Your team could beat his if they wanted to. You said their skills were excellent."

"But boys?"

"You have to do it," she said firmly. "You have to beat them. It's good for Ben to be put in his place once in a while."

Owen grinned and sipped his lemonade. "You sound as if you're feeling better."

"I do. My throat isn't nearly as sore." She drew back

the sleeve of his T-shirt to show the underside of her arms.
Her skin was splotchy with angry, red raised welts against
her pale skin. "But this rash is so gross."

"I think it's pretty attractive." He took her hand and
kissed the pulse of her wrist. "I, personally, like my
women red and scaly."

She laughed and pulled away, studying him carefully.
"Tell the truth. Have you been reading books on how to
seduce women or something?"

"How'd you guess?" He winked. "How am I doing so
far?"

"You're utterly charming." She wrapped her arms
around her knees. "And obviously you've experienced
some success." Her cheeks colored in a most adorable
way and he knew she was thinking about when they'd
made love during the hurricane. "But—"

"There's always the *but,* isn't there?"

"But you forget, Owen Thomas," she continued. "I
know you."

"You know the *old* me," he corrected. "The pre-my-
wife-left-me-because-I-was-a-self-centered-jerk me."

She watched him with the most beautiful blue eyes. But
they were sad eyes that reflected emotional pain, and it
made Owen ache to think he had caused that injury. "What
would you think about giving me another chance?" he
asked quietly.

He took her hand in his again and turned it over,
smoothing her cool palm. He loved her hands. Not just
the way they could touch him. He loved them for the way
they moved, the way they expressed what she was thinking
when she got excited and waved them, wildly. He loved

the way they turned the pages of a book, the way they patted Edgar and made him wag his tail.

She didn't pull away, but she didn't snuggle up against him either. She was not going to be an easy sell. Her pain was real and he knew he had to take responsibility for that pain. He had to pay the price.

She shook her head slowly. "I can't, Owen. I have my book. My dream.

"You could write your book here," he argued. "It's perfect—the house you grew up in, lots of good memories, lots of peace and quiet. I could take care of you so you could work as much as you wanted. My new job is so flexible. I can cook, clean. Just tell me what you want, Abby. I'm here for you. I swear I am. I know I wasn't before, but I am now."

She seemed to want to believe him. He could see it in her eyes, the way she pursed her lips.

"You could have your dream and we could have each other." He rubbed her hand between his. "Don't you see that?"

"Owen—"

"I know what you're thinking." He didn't want to look like a fool, but he wanted to say what he thought. He had to do it now while he still had the courage. "You're thinking I screwed it all up once. You're thinking I'll do it again. Men never change. That's what those women's magazines say. But it's not true. I *have* changed. You know I have."

Tears filled Abby's eyes.

He hated to see her cry. He hated to be the one responsible for those tears.

"You don't understand," she said softly.

He gripped her hand. "I want to. Abby, I'll do anything to make this right with you."

She gazed into his eyes. "You mean that, don't you?"

For a moment, he thought he was going to tear up, too. He loved her so much. "I mean it."

She glanced away. "And what about the guys?"

"What about them?"

"The GAG Club. Bachelors, Inc?"

He frowned. She was still letting him hold her hand, but she was distancing herself emotionally. He could feel it. "Who told you about that?"

"Ben. At his house the other night."

"Jerk," he muttered under his breath.

She chuckled. "Actually, it's pretty funny. The three of you, the lady-killers of Land's End, swearing off women forever."

"They don't understand," he tried to explain. "They've never met anyone they wanted to spend the rest of their life with. They don't understand how I feel about you because they've never been in love like we were . . . like I still am."

There. He did it. He stuck his neck out—hell, he'd stuck out his whole head. The question was, would she chop it off?

Abby made herself pull her hand from Owen's. If she didn't now, she knew she'd end up in his arms again. This time, she'd be lucky if she made it inside to the living room floor. She was such a romantic, such a sap, when it came to sweet talk and promises. And Owen was saying all the right things. He knew what buttons to push on her, not just physically, but emotionally as well.

It would be so easy to say yes. To agree to stay here.

But the divorce—no, what had happened between them before the divorce—had almost ruined her. She couldn't live through that again. . . .

But what if Owen had changed? Her mind was spinning.

He certainly acted as if he had. He had been nothing but attentive since she arrived. He'd been there for her. Wasn't that all she had ever wanted from him in the first place? Wasn't that why she'd left?

"Think about it," Owen said softly in a warm sexy voice that penetrated the wall she was trying so desperately to build between them.

"Just say you'll think about it, please?"

She wanted to think about it. She wanted to say yes, she would give it a try. She wanted to be loved by Owen because she had never stopped loving him. But she didn't want to be stupid either.

"I'll think about it," she finally said softly.

He jumped out of the rocking chair looking like a little boy who had just won box seats to the World Series and the Orioles were American League Champs. "You'll think about it?"

"I said I would think about it. When I feel better," she clarified. "I still feel lousy and I look gross." She gestured. "I can't think when I look gross.

"That's all I'm asking." He leaned over her, pressing his hands to each of the arms of her rocking chair. "Can I have a kiss?"

"You're going to get sick," she warned.

"I'm not. I'm immune. Your undying love protects me from strep throat and plantar warts."

He leaned over and kissed her. It was a soft romantic kiss of promise.

She pushed him away. "I thought you were going running." He had come out onto the porch dressed in a raggedy tee and his running shorts.

"I am."

"Then go." She shooed him. "Go run, take a shower and make me something to eat. I'm going up to the sick room to read. I might even get my computer out."

He stood, realizing he wasn't getting any more kisses. "Five miles and I'll be back."

She tapped her wrist, though she wasn't wearing her watch. "I'll be timing you."

"You better not." He skipped down the steps backward, pulling his knees up high.

"You're going to break your neck," she warned. "And then who will coach the Sox?"

"You." He blew her a kiss and then took off running down the driveway.

Abby hugged her knees, watching him disappear down the street. She was out of her mind. She knew she was out of her mind. She'd been reading too many romance novels where men and women lived happily ever after. It didn't happen in real life. Couples didn't divorce, then remarry and live happily ever after. And if she called Jess, she was certain her friend could provide the statistics.

But Jess wasn't a dreamer. She never had been. Abby was a dreamer. It was what made her writing so real, so vivid, she thought. It was that quality that would lead her down the path to success in her writing career. She was sure of it.

So, why couldn't she dream about living a life happily

ever after with Owen? She'd loved him since the day he'd moved in next door when they were ten.

Abby smiled to herself. She wasn't ready to throw herself into Owen's arms and tell him all was forgiven. She still thought she needed to go to the cottage, spend some time working and thinking, but for the first time she was beginning to consider that maybe there was hope.

Maybe she and Owen had just gotten sidetracked. Maybe she hadn't lost him after all.

Eleven

The following day Abby sat down at Owen's desk and punched Jess's phone number at work. Her secretary connected them.

"Jessica Morgan."

"Hey, it's Abby." She fiddled with the phone cord. "Just checking in."

"Abby! I'm so glad you called." She spoke in her high-powered executive voice. "I was worried about you. I called several times last night and you never picked up."

Abby twisted the cord around her finger. "You called here?"

"I called the cottage," Jess said tersely. "Where's *here?*"

Abby had known this was coming, of course. "I'm still at Owen's."

"You've got to be kidding!" Jess shrieked. "Please don't tell me he seduced you. Please don't tell me you're sliding down the slippery slope into 'use em and bruise 'em' ex-husband land."

"I have strep throat. The doctor said I can't travel." Abby spotted where she had written her name on Owen's blotter. She smiled when she saw the heart he'd drawn around their names. How sweet. Who said men couldn't be romantic?

"You couldn't be taken by ambulance to Myrtle Beach?"

Abby laughed. "Very funny. Listen, I'm fine. I just wanted you to know where I am so you wouldn't worry about me or the house."

"To hell with the house. I'm just concerned about you. The man's got you in his lair and you're sick. Anything could happen."

Abby thought about the *anything* that had happened the other afternoon on the living room floor. She wouldn't confess her secret to Jess, of course. But she kept finding herself going back to that afternoon, reliving it in seat-wiggling detail. There was no doubt about it, Owen had lost none of his sex appeal.

"I'm on antibiotics," Abby said, tracing Owen's name with her fingertip. "I'm already feeling better."

"Want me to come? I've got plenty of vacation time and no one to go to Aruba with. I can drive you to the beach if you're not up to it."

"No, don't be silly." It was on the tip of her tongue to say that Owen had been wonderful. That he was a far better nurse than she was, but she was afraid Jess would launch into another anti-Owen diatribe. "Hopefully, I should be well enough to travel by the weekend. I've just got this nasty rash now." She scratched her arm. "I don't want anyone thinking I have leprosy."

"So, you'll be there by Sunday?"

"I don't know," Abby hedged. "It just depends."

"On what?"

"On when I decide to go," Abby said firmly. "You're not my keeper, Jess."

"Well, you need one."

Abby made no response and Jess sighed on the other end. When she spoke again, the corporate executive was gone and it was her good friend speaking. Her tone softened. "I'm sorry. I'm not trying to pick on you, babe. It's just that I've been there. I made the mistake of going back and I can tell you that it hurt a hell of a lot more the second time around."

Abby smiled sadly, hearing the pain Jess hid so well. She had loved her husband, too, and now her college professor ex-husband was married to one of his students, twenty-two and bleached blond with a tattoo on her butt. "I understand," she said simply. And she did. Jess was just like Zack and Ben, cut from the same mold. Good friends, though misguided. They were only trying to protect those they loved. None of them could believe two people who met in the fourth grade could actually be meant for each other.

"Well, I've got to run. Meeting at four with the brass, but you call me if you need me. OK?"

"OK."

"And no one last screw for old time's sake, promise me?"

Abby grinned. There was one thing she could say about Jess; she never minced words. "Hanging up now," she said sweetly.

"Later, girlfriend."

Abby no sooner hung up the phone, when it rang. She picked it up. "Hello?"

"Birth control." It was Jess.

Abby laughed. "I never stopped taking my pills. You know me, I need the hormones. Stop worrying!"

"Just checking . . ."

Abby was setting the phone on the cradle the second time when Owen came in the front door, Edgar right behind him. He'd been out walking the dog. Edgar grabbed his leash from his master's hand and padded into the kitchen. The Bernese would leave the leash on the bench in the laundry room, ready for their next outing.

"I'm getting ready to go to softball practice." Owen adjusted the brim of his new Red Sox ball cap. "Want to come?"

"I don't know." She walked into the hall. "I guess I could; I'm not contagious anymore."

"Sure. You've been on the antibiotics long enough."

She wrinkled her nose. She did feel like getting out. "How long is the practice? I still don't have a lot of energy yet. This thing has really whipped me."

"Just an hour," he said quickly. "And if you get tired, you can wait in the car." He smiled sheepishly from under the brim of his cap. "I'd really like you to meet my girls."

He said my girls; how could she resist him? "OK," she said. "Just let me run up and grab my sunglasses."

The Red Sox were waiting in the dugout for Owen when he and Abby arrived at the field. They were so cute, lined up on the bench, dressed in various outfits they saw fit to practice in. Many were wearing shorts and tees and ball caps or floppy hats. But one had a ballet tutu and sneakers on, another, a fringed skirt and cowboy boots. One girl was wearing a wide-brimmed straw hat with flowers she'd obviously glued on herself.

Owen grabbed the equipment from his trunk. "Come on," he said, waving to her. "You can help me out. I'm really not very good with kids."

Abby climbed out of the car. "Give yourself a chance. I'll just hang back and watch. Maybe spy a little for the competition."

He flashed her a grin that made her realize she was dangerously close to climbing into his bed again . . . and enjoying every moment of it. She had never been able to resist that grin of his.

"Hey, guys!" Owen called. "Um, girls . . ."

The little girls laughed.

Owen dropped the equipment bag on the floor of the dugout and fished out a clipboard. "Just let me check off who's here and we'll get started." He began to call names.

"Tonesha."

"Here." A little girl in an Orioles ball cap that was two sizes too big for her waved.

"Kari."

"She's still at tap dancing."

"Monica."

"Here." The tutu waved.

Owen frowned and moved on.

Abby couldn't resist a chuckle. She knew what he was thinking. No one on Ben or Zack's practice field would be late because he was taking dance class. But Owen was being a good sport.

"Tiffany."

"Here." She adjusted one of the flowers on her straw hat.

"Whitney."

"In the potty."

Abby watched him grimace and hesitate, then check off Whitney's name and move down the roster. "Nell."

A big girl wearing shin guards and a ball cap backward waved. "Here, Coach."

Owen made it through the rest of the names. "Now, guys . . . I mean girls," he stumbled.

"It's OK, Coach. You can call us guys," Nell piped up. "We'll still answer." She wrinkled her freckled nose. "I have four big brothers so I'm used to it."

Owen clapped his hands. "Let's do some warm-ups and get rolling. The season opening is only a week away. We've got a lot of ground to cover before then."

Abby watched from the fence as the girls followed him to the grassy outfield. He led them in a series of exercises, but Abby could see right away that it wasn't going the way he wanted it to. The girls kept interrupting his instructions to tell each other what color nail polish they bought at the Big Mart and who spent the night at whose house the previous night. Between stretches they started impromptu clapping games accompanied by song.

"Girls, girls, let's try to focus," Owen said in frustration. "Warm-ups are important. They prevent injuries during practice and games."

Several team members smiled apologetically at him . . . and went right on chattering.

From the chain-link fence, Abby tried to hide her amusement. She didn't want Owen to think she wasn't being supportive, but it was funny to see him struggle. He had always been the kind of man who needed to be in control.

Next, Owen lined the girls up to face each other and they played catch. Actually, they attempted to play catch. Whitney returned from the bathroom to hit Monica in the head with a softball three times before Monica, clad in her pink tutu, took aim and returned fire, striking Whitney in the chest so hard that she knocked her over. Owen ran to be sure neither girl was hurt, and Tonesha threw her ball over the fence into the boys' field. While Tonesha climbed the fence and hollered nonsense at the boys, Tiffany wandered off to sit on the bleachers, and several girls took a break and sat down to make grass-chain bracelets.

"Girls!" Owen called to his scattered team.

No one responded.

"Girls, practice isn't over yet." He waved his hands, nearly in despair. "Girls?"

He looked so pathetic that Abby came through the gate. "Need a little help?" she asked, her tone teasing.

He looked as if she'd just thrown him a life jacket. "Maybe four hands would be better than two?"

Abby clapped her hands and hollered with authority. "Ladies, let's get rolling here."

"Who's that, Coach?" Nell tugged on the hem of Owen's shirt. "Your girlfriend?"

"This is my assistant, Coach Thomas," Owen introduced Abby diplomatically.

"But aren't you Coach Thomas?" Nell peered up at him.

"I'm Coach Abby." She waved to the girl on the bleachers.

The girl waved back cheerfully.

"I'll get her. She can be thick, but she's a good player." Nell took off.

Within five minutes Abby had all the girls assembled again. "What next?" she asked Owen, hands balanced on her hips.

"I think we need to go over our throwing skills."

Abby put out her hands. "Nell, toss me your glove."

The girl tossed it.

"Okay, ladies, have a seat in the grass. Listen up and watch while Coach Owen shows us how to throw the ball. There will be a test afterward."

The girls giggled.

Owen and Abby separated and Owen reviewed the basics of the correct way to throw a softball. As he talked and demonstrated, Abby added tidbits of information when she thought his terms were too technical.

"Just pretend you're a scarecrow," Abby told the girls. "See?" She spread her arms in slow motion, turning sideways, then threw the ball back to Owen. It made a popping sound as it hit his glove.

"Nice throw," he said.

She smiled. "Thank you. I guess there are some things we don't forget."

After that demonstration followed by one on catching, they practiced their skills, again lining up and facing each other. This time the team met with far more success.

Half an hour later, the girls were running to their parents' minivans and Owen was loading the equipment into his car.

Abby waved as the last girl was picked up. "Bye, Tonesha. Practice that scarecrow."

Owen shook his head as they got into the car. "Thank God you came," he said, thrusting the key into the ignition. "I couldn't have gotten through that without you."

"Sure you could have." She patted his knee. "You just have to get into the swing of things. This is your first coaching experience."

"No. I don't know how to talk to them. They're just so different than the boys. They think so differently." He eyed her. "We don't wear pink ruffly stuff on the ball field."

She laughed. "So, change the way you think. Coach to them, not to Zack or Ben's team. They can learn the skills just as well as boys their age; they just learn differently."

He gripped the steering wheel. "How are they ever going to be ready to play in another week?" he groaned. "We're going to get creamed."

"I think you're wrong. Tonesha has an incredible arm."

"But no aim. She threw it over the fence into the other field for heaven's sake. She almost took Zack's right fielder's head off."

"Nell seems to inherently understand the game, and Tiffany may be ditzy but she can knock the cover off a softball."

"If you're so confident of the team's ability, why don't you stay and help me?" He glanced at her sideways, then returned his gaze to the road.

She patted his knee. "Good try. Excellent. Sneaky. But no good. I'm going to the cottage and I'm going to write my book."

He shrugged, seeming to sense he needed to keep the conversation light. "You can't blame a guy for trying."

She watched out the window as familiar scenery whizzed by; it was a comforting feeling.

"Why don't we stop at the grocery store, pick up a few

things and I'll whip up some dinner for you?" Owen asked. "Afterward, you could work and I could get something done on the McClusky blueprints. We've got a meeting next week and I have to be ready for the big sell. I'd like you to see them. You always had a good eye for this kind of thing."

"Sounds like a plan."

Inside the grocery store, Owen pushed the cart while Abby made their selections. As they shopped, they talked and laughed, about nothing in particular. It was fun, like the old days when they were first married and living on peanut butter and love. It amazed Abby how easy it was to talk to Owen now. Before she left, their communication had dwindled to who picked up the mail and whether or not they needed skim milk. She wondered if it was the time apart that made it so easy to talk again, or if Owen had really changed as much as he said he had. Had he really become the man she had fallen in love with once again?

They were wheeling down the fruit and vegetable aisle, discussing the plot of a really bad B movie they both loved when they spotted Max. He was accompanied by a woman who appeared to be in her mid-fifties—a good twenty years younger than Max. They were walking arm and arm, pushing the cart together, their heads together like two love birds.

"Max!" Abby called.

He waited for them to catch up. "Abby and Owen, I want you to meet a friend. This is Phyllis."

Phyllis was dressed smartly in a designer skirt and blouse, her heavily highlighted hair cut in a fashionable style. Big gold earrings hung from her ears and she wore frosted pink lipstick.

"It's so nice to meet you," Phyllis gushed. She pumped Abby's hand, then Owen's before latching on to Max again. "Any friend of Max's is a friend of mine," she cooed.

"I'm making dinner," Max explained. "We're just doing a little shopping."

Phyllis ran her hand up and down Max's suntanned arm. "The sly fox is just trying to get me into the sack." She kissed his cheek. "It's working, too."

Owen met Abby's gaze, his eyes wide with surprise. She glanced away to keep from giggling. Owen cleared his throat. "Well, I guess we'd better let you get back to shopping." He looked to Max. "But I wanted to thank you for not carrying tales to the guys. About you know—" He nodded at Abby. "Her being at the house."

"I already told you what I think, boy. She belongs in that house. You belong there together." He winked at Abby. "What Zack and Ben know about love would fill a thimble." He gave a nod. "I just want to see the two of you happy again, that's all."

Abby blushed and reached for a fresh tomato on display. She didn't know how she felt about Max and Owen discussing hers and Owen's relationship or lack thereof.

Max and his date wheeled off and Owen came to stand beside her. "The guys came by while you were asleep yesterday and interrogated me," he explained.

"About my still being there, I suppose?" She turned the tomato in her hand.

"They're just trying to help. Anyway, I thought maybe Max had told them that you were there, because I hadn't," he continued. "But he was innocent. The guys saw your car."

She selected two tomatoes, put them in the cart and pushed it forward. "So, you and Max talked about me when he came by?"

"Then and that night at Ben's. We talked about us, not you. I hope you don't mind. Let me do that." He pushed the cart for her. "I've always respected Max's opinion."

Again, her feelings were in a jumble. She didn't know what to think. Owen was actually seeking advice from someone older and wiser rather than his buddies, Dumb and Dumber? "So, what was Max's take on the situation?"

"You heard him. He thinks we were meant for each other."

She narrowed her eyes, grabbing a cantaloupe. "You pay him to say that?"

He leaned toward her, bringing his nose close to hers. "Face it," he whispered. "We are meant for each other. We just got sidetracked. *I* got sidetracked."

She tried not to smile, but she couldn't keep it back. She could smell his aftershave; he was wearing her favorite. His words made her feel warm all over. Maybe it was just the rash, but she doubted it. "You're such a shmuck." She gently brought her palm to his cheek. "I suppose you intend to buy wine, too, just to loosen me up, get me into your bed again."

His gaze held hers. "If it would work, I'd buy a winery."

A part of her shouted "run away," but a part was enjoying this sexy repartee. And why shouldn't she enjoy it? She was a thirty-something woman in the company of a man for whom, despite their differences, she cared a great deal. And he had been her husband once upon a time. Didn't that count for something?

She walked away from him. "Go for the wine," she told him over her shoulder, feeling sexier than she had in years. "I have a feeling you might just get lucky."

Twelve

Abby and Owen shared a simple supper of salad, freshly made bruschetta and a glass of wine, then went their separate ways. Owen worked in his office on his new blueprints while Abby sat cross-legged on her bed with her laptop. She wrote the first four pages of her prologue and was thrilled with the first draft.

Smiling to herself, she went downstairs to find Owen. She halted in the doorway to watch him at his drafting table. He was playing classical music on the stereo, and concentrating so heavily on his work that he didn't hear her enter the room.

Edgar lifted his head with interest, then let it drop, closing his eyes again.

Just standing in the doorway watching Owen made her warm all over. Maybe it was the sulfites in the red wine.

Maybe it was Owen.

It was so good to see him enthusiastic about his work again. That was how he had been in college and when he first started at Jacob & Jacob. But somehow he had lost that love of his craft in the midst of battling for offices with windows and a healthy expense account.

She walked up behind him and laid her hands on his shoulders. Such broad muscular shoulders. Many runners had weak upper bodies, but not Owen. Not anymore at least. He seemed to understand the importance of balance now. Maybe in his life too.

He looked up, smiling. "So, how'd it go?"

She smiled back. "Good. Better than good. I started the prologue."

"Can I read it?"

She knitted her brows. "No."

"Will you dedicate it to me?"

"No."

He turned in his drafting stool to slip his arm around her waist. "Make wild passionate love to me?"

"Owen!" She laughed and gave him a push, but secretly she was flattered . . . and amused. Her mother had always said one of the most important attributes in a husband was his ability to make his wife laugh.

"Just asking."

She let him continue to hold her. "So, what's up with the blueprint?"

"I'm trying to figure out how to add this three-car garage without altering the look of the original structure, but it's a bear."

She studied the plans carefully. "So, you're trying to keep the basic shape, while still making the new space convenient?"

He nodded. "Exactly."

They talked about his blueprint for several minutes and she made a few suggestions that he seemed to appreciate. Then they drifted into the kitchen to refill the wineglasses they'd left on the counter.

He poured her a glass and handed it to her. "I really had a good day today," he said quietly.

"So did I." She sipped her wine. It was a pungent Merlot that glided down her throat.

He stared at the hardwood floor at her feet, then slowly lifted his gaze until it was level with hers. His blue eyes were open and honest. "I think we make a good pair, Abby, two halves that make a great whole."

She watched him, measuring the sincerity in his voice. He was utterly sincere. "That's a very romantic thing to say," she said, her own voice sultry.

"Maybe." He lifted his shoulder. "But it's true." He stared into his wine, then at her again. "I want you to give me a second chance. Or at least consider it."

"Do we have to talk about this now?" She ran her finger around the rim of the glass and touched it to her lips.

He took a step closer. "If I didn't know better, I would think you were trying to seduce me."

She laughed. "I was just going to say the same thing."

He slipped his hand around her waist and brought his lips to hers. It was a gentle kiss, one of promise. "I thought women wanted to talk everything out. Get their feelings, their hopes and dreams out into the open," he said against her mouth.

"They do," she whispered, gazing up into his eyes, feeling wicked and sexy. "But haven't you ever heard that there's a time and a place for everything?"

"I take it this isn't the time for talking."

She held his gaze, her lips slightly parted, tasting the wine from the lips of the only man she had ever loved. "You're taking it right."

He slipped his hand into hers and side by side, in silence, they climbed the stairs. They passed her bedroom and went into his.

"I haven't exactly got around to getting a real bed yet," he said sheepishly as he flipped on the overhead light.

She sipped her wine and glanced at the king-sized mattress and box springs on a metal frame. No headboard or footboard. It was covered in paisley sheets and a comforter. "That never stopped us before, did it?"

He laughed and came to stand in front of her, resting one hand on her hip. They both still held their wineglasses. "Do you remember that first bed, right after we were married?" he asked with amusement.

She chuckled. "Your parents had it in their attic, saving it for a yard sale."

"No box spring, just a mattress."

She grinned. "Didn't slow us down a bit, did it?"

He brushed his lips against hers. "And we didn't have far to fall when we rolled off, did we?"

"No."

He kissed her and slipped out of her arms. "Hold that thought."

She watched as he moved around the room, lighting strategically placed candles. They smelled like vanilla. Her favorite.

"Did you have this planned?" she asked, amused and flattered at the same time.

"Let's just say I'm a wishful thinker." He flipped off the overhead light and returned to her. Placing both of their glasses on the table beside the bed, he wrapped his arms around her waist and lowered his mouth to hers.

Abby took his tongue into her mouth and this time their

kiss was more forceful, each demanding more of the other. When they parted, she was breathless, warm and flushed.

He ran his hand down her back, his fingers tracing the hollow. "I've always loved your back," he said softly. "The way it curves. How soft the skin is, how I can trace the bumps of your spine."

"The bumps of my spine? Now that's sexy," she teased. But as she spoke she turned around, presenting her back to him. Taking her time, she slipped her shirt over her head and let it glide to the floor.

He slid both hands slowly down her back and planted a kiss on the nape of her neck, below her ponytail. She shivered with pleasure.

Letting her eyes drift shut, enjoying the sensation of his hands on her skin, she unhooked her bra at the front and slipped out of it as well.

"Abby," Owen whispered, drawing her closer. He slid his hands over her hips, around to her waist and slowly upward to cup her breasts.

She leaned against him, bathing in the warmth that seemed to radiate from his fingertips. "Junior size," she apologized.

His breath was warm in her ear. "The perfect size. Made just for me."

She laughed as she turned to face him.

"I love to hear you laugh like that."

She almost felt embarrassed by his compliments. But this was how Owen had once been before work took over his life. Abby knew she wasn't the most beautiful woman on earth, but he had always made her feel as if she was. "You love to hear me laugh like what?"

"The way you do when we're making love." His voice

was as soft a caress as his hands on her breasts. "Deep in your throat. It's so sexy and sweet at the same time."

She laughed against his shoulder and lifted her chin to meet his mouth.

"There it is again," he said against her lips.

She grabbed the hem of his tee shirt and pulled it over his head, dropping it on the floor with hers. She loved to feel her breasts against the crisp hair of his chest. "There, that's better."

Their mouths met again and she pressed her groin against his, enjoying the feel of his hardness against her curves.

Abby could hear the faint music that still played from downstairs. Bach. The candles flickered and the scent of vanilla was subtle in the air. Owen had created the perfect atmosphere, just for her.

He brushed back the locks of hair that had fallen from her ponytail and kissed her cheek, the tip of her nose, the point of her chin. "I think you'd be more comfortable without these." He rested his hands on her hips and tucked his thumbs into the waistband of her shorts.

"Oh, yeah? Well I think you'd be more comfortable without these." She caught his shorts with both hands and slid them down, taking his boxers with them.

Owen stepped out of his shorts and tossed them to the floor with the flip of one bare foot. He took his time in removing hers, sliding them down slowly.

Abby closed her eyes, enjoying the feel of the denim fabric as it brushed over her skin, followed by the touch of his fingers. As he slid them over her hips, he lowered himself slowly to the floor.

She sighed as he kissed her bare belly, first above her

navel then below. She rested her hands on his shoulders, feeling dizzy with anticipation.

He slid his warm mouth lower.

"Don't you want to get into bed?" she whispered, intoxicated by his touch.

"I'm comfortable here if you are."

She wrapped her arms around his neck and moaned softly as his mouth met the bed of curls at the apex of her thighs. She felt her shorts slide down her legs to puddle at her ankles.

Owen caressed her calves, the backs of her knees, all the while doing clever little things with the tip of his tongue.

She couldn't keep her eyes open. She swayed, weak at the knees as waves of pleasure washed over her.

"I'm going to fall over," she laughed.

"I'll catch you," he whispered.

"Owen!" she protested lightly as he climbed to his knees, cupping her buttocks with his warm firm hands. But she had no intentions of telling him to stop. This was too wonderful.

He kissed her again and again, his tongue darting out, flicking, laving.

Abby felt herself spinning, twirling, like a top turning in tighter and tighter circles. She threaded her fingers through Owen's hair, wanting to hold back and make the sensations last forever, but needing release.

Her orgasm came hard and fast and she threw her head back and cried out. Owen rose up until he was on his feet again and held her in his arms as tremors of pleasure still washed over her.

"Bed now?" he whispered in her ear.

"Before I fall over."

He surprised her by picking her up; he really was a romantic. She rested her cheek on his bare shoulder, looping her arms around his neck as he carried her. He lowered her onto the bed on top of the comforter and lay down beside her.

"I've missed you so much. Missed this." He ran his hand down her side, dipping in at her waist, gliding up over her hip, down her thigh.

"I've missed you, too," she confessed, brushing her hand over his chest, enjoying the planes of his muscles.

He lowered his head over hers and their mouths met. Abby rested one hand on his waist and tugged, urging him over her. She needed him, needed to feel him inside her. She parted her thighs and flexed her hips, unable to suppress a moan as he brushed against her leg, hot and hard.

"Owen," she begged.

He buried his face in the hollow between her shoulder and her neck and slipped inside her. She rose up to meet him with a cry of pleasure, of relief. They began to move, rocking slowly at first, than faster. Her breath caught in her throat again and again. Every artery, every vein in her body seemed to be rushing, hot and quick.

Owen knew how to bring her to the edge of the cliff only to draw her back again. He knew how to tease, how to taunt. He knew what she liked, how she liked it.

Abby grabbed the pillow beneath her head and gripped it in her fists, lifting her hips to meet his. Every muscle in her body, every fiber of her being tightened and then she felt herself falling, falling in bliss, crying out his name.

Owen thrust once more, groaned with his own release and then lowered his cheek to her breast, panting.

After a moment, he rolled onto his side and drew her against him. She was hot and sweaty and her entire body still tingled with delicious sensation.

"I was thinking about going sailing tomorrow after practice. Want to go?" he asked when they could speak again.

"Sailing?" She settled her head on the pillow. "I don't know. I suppose I should think about packing."

He gazed into her eyes. "Oh, come on, please, Ab? I want you to see my new Sailfish. We could take a picnic lunch. I know this little island. Completely uninhabited," he whispered huskily in her ear. "Completely private."

She cut her eyes at him. "Are you trying to seduce me again when these sheets are still warm?"

He raised one hand innocently. "Just offering the options."

Abby didn't have to think about his offer. She didn't know what she thought about him asking her to stay, but she did know she'd love to go sailing with him. It had been one of their favorite pastimes in their earlier days. "All right, sailing it is.

"Great! I'll be home from practice by five."

Abby immediately felt a twinge of wariness. Owen stating a time when he would be home was dangerous. In the last days of their marriage he had become completely undependable. But he had changed, hadn't he? She could depend on him. He certainly wouldn't screw this up.

"You better be. Otherwise we'll be sailing home in the dark."

He kissed her cheek in the sweetest gesture. "You know I love you, Abby."

"I know," she breathed, as she stared at the shadows of the Casablanca fan dancing on the ceiling.

"If I were a greedier man, that wouldn't be enough." He traced the line of her jaw. "But it's enough for me, Abby. It's enough for now. All I'm looking for is a crumb of hope."

She turned her head to look him in the eyes. "Whether I loved you was never an issue, Owen," she answered, her heart open to him. "You know I always have, always will."

"That mean I get a second chance?" he whispered, holding her tight.

Her eyes drifted shut as she smiled to herself. "I thought you weren't a greedy man."

He kissed her cheek. "I'm not."

She chuckled, snuggling against him. "No, you're not. Just a persistent one."

Thirteen

Abby leaned against the kitchen counter and checked her watch. It was two minutes later than the last time she'd checked it. She bit down on her lower lip, fighting the old insecurities that were coming back all too quickly.

It was only 5:20. Owen was only twenty minutes late. Anything could make a person twenty minutes late, she reasoned. A flat tire, a concerned parent, a quick stop at the grocery store. He *was* low on milk.

She glanced at the picnic basket resting on the center of the kitchen table. She had packed Granny Smith apples and sharp cheddar cheese, cold salmon and crackers for their sailing excursion. On impulse, she had added two old wineglasses, a bottle of Chardonnay she'd found in one of the kitchen cabinets and a beach blanket. In the old days they had made love on the beach after sailing and a picnic.

She glanced at her watch again. 5:22. Where was he? She was sure he had said he would be home by five.

She walked to the back door through the laundry room and gazed out the window into the yard. Edgar was sleeping under a tree. Earlier today, after writing six more pages of her novel, she had cleaned her bedroom and the bathroom. Edgar had followed her around, just as he had in the old days. Though at first she'd been amused, eventually he'd become such a pest that she had chased him out of the bathroom and the dog had retreated to Owen's room to sulk. Later, she'd fed him a dog treat and let him outside. He seemed to have recovered now.

She let the curtain on the back door fall and walked back into the kitchen. It was almost 5:30 now. Half an hour late. People weren't ordinarily half an hour late without reason.

She walked over to the table, lifted the lid of the picnic basket and peered inside. Everything was just as she had left it. She let the lid fall with a snap.

She groaned aloud.

No matter how she tried to fight them, thoughts of the past slipped into her head. She remembered evenings waiting for Owen, dinner on the stove, on the table, in the microwave, so she could warm it up when he finally got home. Sometimes he'd called, but sometimes he hadn't. He was apologetic when it first started, then later he said she should expect him to be late. Eventually, she stopped making dinner.

It wasn't the dinner that had been so important, or that she had come home after a long day at work to cook for them. It was the fact that he wasn't there to talk to her that had gotten to her. He wasn't there to hear how her day had gone. He wasn't there to listen to her complain about her job, about the people she worked with. He wasn't there to hear about her accomplishments. He just wasn't there for her.

She walked into the front hall, her sneakers squeaking on the wooden floor. It was 5:40.

Why the hell doesn't he call?

She went into the living room and turned on the small TV in a console against the wall. She flipped through the channels: a game show, afternoon cartoons, several talk shows. She turned it off and wandered out of the room.

It was six o'clock. Soon it would be too late to sail very far. Owen had said he wanted to take her to a little island he had found where they would picnic.

Standing in the hallway, she glanced at the phone. Had he been involved in an automobile accident? That was what she had wondered the first few times he'd worked late at the office and forgotten to call.

She wondered if she should call Zack or Ben. Maybe they had heard from him.

She spun on her heels, grimacing. Over her dead body . . .

At 6:15, she unpacked the picnic basket. Her eyes burned and a lump rose in her throat. She had set herself up for this. There was no use feeling sorry for herself.

But last night, wrapped in Owen's arms, everything had been so perfect, felt so right. She had almost been convinced that he had changed. He had almost had her believing they could work things out between them.

Fool. Fool. She'd always been a pushover when it came to Owen.

Abby was climbing the steps at 6:30 when she heard Owen's car pull into the driveway. She was at the top of the landing when he burst through the door. "Abby!"

She hesitated on the step, wanting to just go to her room

and pack, not wanting a confrontation. She hated confrontations.

"There you are." He pulled off his Red Sox cap. "I'm so sorry I'm late."

"Not a problem." She turned into the hallway, headed for her room.

He bounded up the stairs two at a time. "Are you upset with me?" He sounded surprised.

"Why would I be upset with you?" She walked into her room and grabbed her duffel bag off the floor.

He halted in the doorway, filling it. He watched her. "You *are* upset. Why are you upset?"

He really seemed to not have a clue. Typical. "You told me five o'clock," she said quietly. She would not shout. She would not cry.

"I know. Practice ended at 4:30, right on time. I was going to be back in plenty of time, then—"

"You don't have to give me an explanation." She threw the bag onto the bed and began to stuff neatly folded clean clothes into it.

"What are you doing?" He stepped into the room. The old polished floorboards creaked under his size twelve sneakers.

"Packing."

"You can't do that," he said, incredulous. "We'll go tomorrow. You can put the drive off another day.

She shook her head. "This wasn't a good idea. I'm sorry." What was she apologizing for? "I really need to go."

"Abby!" He lifted his hands, then let them fall to his sides as if he were helpless. "I know what you're thinking. Owen's late again, the inconsiderate jerk."

"I didn't say that." She grabbed her make-up bag and tossed it on top of her running shorts.

"Don't you even want to know why I was late?"

She continued packing.

"Lilly's parents never came for her. We waited and waited. Then I took her home, but no one was there. We ended up calling her grandparents and I had to run her out there. It was way out in the country."

It was too late for explanations. It wasn't that she didn't believe him. She just couldn't take this. This week it would be a perfectly logical explanation; within a month, there would be none at all.

"Abby." He brushed her arm, his fingertips hot on her skin. "Why won't you talk to me?"

"You could have called," she said without emotion. As long as she stayed calm, she wouldn't cry and make a fool of herself in front of him.

"I did."

She glared at him. "The phone never rang. I waited for a call."

He sighed with exasperation. "It's been busy. I thought maybe you were killing time on the Internet while you were waiting for me. If I'd known you were worried—"

"I *wasn't* worried."

He strode out of the room.

So, was that it? She stared at the empty doorway in disbelief.

She heard him go down the hall into his room. Typical. He had always walked away rather than discuss their problems.

She wiped at her scratchy eyes with the back of her hand. Maybe it was better this way.

But less than a minute later, he was back again. "Edgar."

She didn't turn to face him. She felt as if she was crumbling inside. "Pardon?"

"Edgar. Edgar knocked the phone off the hook in my bedroom. He does it all the time. That's why I don't let him in there."

The dog *had* been in the bedroom—when she'd been cleaning the bathroom. But it was too late. She was already hardening inside, telling herself there were a million reasons not to trust him. People didn't change. Hadn't she read that in all the self-help books she had bought after they separated? Wasn't that what Jess was trying to tell her on the phone?

"It's really better if I just go tomorrow," she said quietly.

He stood in the doorway again, watching her with those big blue eyes of his—eyes she had gazed into last night when they'd made love. He looked like Edgar when she'd kicked him out of the bathroom earlier. Truly pathetic.

"I can't believe you're doing this," Owen said.

"Doing what?" She crammed dirty socks in the bag. Her hands were shaky. She was feeling flushed.

"I thought things were going well between us. I thought—"

"I never said I was staying, Owen. *I never said it.*"

"I know, but—"

She spun around. "But what? I jumped into bed with you? That meant I was moving in? Doing your laundry again?"

"That's unfair," he said quietly. He sounded hurt. Lost.

"You never even asked me why I left!" she shouted, throwing up her hands.

God, where had that come from?

Owen blinked. He looked at her. Looked at the floor. "I—"

For an instant, she felt a glimmer of hope. She knew they couldn't go back and change the past, but maybe, just maybe he could shed some light on it. "You what?"

He shook his head and turned away. "Never mind."

Never mind. Of course. Never mind meant it didn't matter. Meant she didn't matter.

Abby turned her back so that she wouldn't see him go. Then she closed the door behind him and shed her tears in private.

After a fitful night of tossing and turning, Owen woke as the light of dawn seeped under the shades of his bedroom windows. He felt like crap. His throat was raw and his head was pounding with every beat of his heart.

Or was that his heart pounding with every beat of his head?

Abby had not come out of her room last night and he hadn't had the guts to go back in again. He had wandered around the house, feeling totally dejected, then turned in early without supper. All evening he kept hearing what she had said over and over in his head. She said he had never even asked her why she left.

The thing was, she was right. He hadn't for a million reasons, none of them good. He knew why she left. He didn't want to hear it confirmed. He didn't have the guts to ask, to hear the truth spoken aloud. It was his pride, too.

But it had never occurred to him that he had hurt her

by not asking. Even when they were going through the divorce, when he was so angry that he hated to see her, even then, he had not wanted to hurt her. Not any more than he already had.

So, why hadn't he asked her last night? It was his damned pride again, of course. It was hard enough on a man when the woman he loved walked out on him, but to have her go without an explanation—it had been more than he had been able to handle at the time.

When he looked back now he realized it was a wonder he'd been handling anything. Work had gotten beyond crazy. It had been insane. He had felt like a rat running on a wheel in a cage. No matter how hard he ran, or how fast, he never got anywhere. He and Abby had had such wonderful plans, a home, vacations in the Caribbean, a sailboat. All he had wanted to do was give her those things.

Yeah, right. He ran his hand through his hair. It was damp with sweat. He kicked off the sheet and lay there in his boxers.

Who was he kidding? He had wanted to succeed so that he could say he was a success. Sure, it would have been nice for him and Abby to have the freedom that kind of money would have provided, but he knew that what he had really wanted was to be able to come back to Land's End with physical proof of his accomplishments; a Lexus, a Rolex watch, diamonds on Abby's fingers. He had wanted those material things, and he'd wanted his dad to be proud of him.

After Abby left, the material things had quickly lost their appeal. Then, on a trip back to Land's End, he had talked with his father and come to the realization that what

his dad wanted was for him to be happy. To his dad, that
was success, not diamonds and sailboats or fifty thousand
dollars' worth of car. Once those realizations sunk in, it
wasn't long before Owen realized he didn't need his name
in gold on the company letterhead. He didn't even need
Boston. Instead of sailing home to Land's End in a yacht,
he had limped home in his Honda sedan.

Owen closed his eyes, listening to the quiet of the
house, hoping to hear Abby stirring. He wanted to tell her
he was sorry. He wanted to let her have her say, to tell
him why she left, face-to-face. It was what he needed to
do. He didn't want her to leave, but if she was going to
go, he at least owed her that much. Maybe he owed it to
himself, too.

Tired and feeling lonelier than he ever had in his life,
Owen got up to take his shower.

Abby zipped up her duffel bag and dropped it onto the
bed. She would have some tea and a piece of toast and
be on her way. She was resigned. All she had to do was
get through the good-bye downstairs and then she'd be
home free. Once she got into her car with her laptop,
headed south for the cottage and her life as a novelist,
everything would be all right.

Yeah, right.

She walked to the closed door and stared at the panels,
breathing deeply. She felt as if she'd been hit by a freight
train. All night she'd lain in bed, thinking of all the things
she should have done, should have said over the years.
No matter how she tried, she knew she couldn't blame

Owen entirely for their break-up. Yes, Owen had ignored her, but she'd let him.

She opened the door with a sadness she'd not known she possessed and went downstairs. She found Owen hovering over the stove, waiting for the teakettle to boil.

As he turned around, she did a double take. "You look awful," she said.

"Thanks."

She went to him and put her hand on his forehead. His face was red and a slight bead of perspiration hung above his upper lip. He had showered, but his hair was messy, his clothes rumpled. It was so unlike him. His head was actually hot to her touch. "You're burning up."

"I took some aspirin."

"Your head hurts?"

He nodded.

"Your throat?" she asked suspiciously.

He looked at her gloomily. "Feels like it's on fire."

She let her hand fall. "You've got strep."

The kettle whistled and he slid it off the burner. "No, I don't."

She rolled her eyes. "Yes, you do." She pushed his hands aside and began to make the pot of tea herself. "Go get some shoes on, I'm taking you over to the hospital."

"The hospital?" He looked at her as if he didn't quite understand.

She dropped her hand to her hip. "Do you have a family physician?"

He stared at her for a second. "Um, no. Doc Edmundson retired. I've been meaning to find someone, but—"

"It's like you told me. It makes more sense to run over to the ER and see someone there than to try and get a physician in town to see you on a Sunday. All you need is a throat culture for a definite diagnosis and an antibiotic."

He swallowed and she could tell it hurt. He blinked. "I can drive myself."

"Owen," she said with a sigh. "You barely know what planet you're on. You're in no condition to drive."

He leaned against the counter and rested his forehead in his hand for a moment, then looked up again. "I thought you wanted to head south this morning."

She kept her gaze fixed on the boiling water she was pouring into the ceramic teapot. "You want me to go?" she said softly.

He was beside her in an instant. He didn't touch her, but he was so close she could feel his body heat. "You know I don't."

She paused. There was so much meaning in his words, meaning she didn't know if she could deal with right this minute. "You're sick. I can't let you drive yourself." She set down the kettle and put the lid on the pot to let the tea steep. "Besides, this is my fault to begin with. I gave you the bug."

When he didn't respond she looked up at his face. He was watching her with those blue eyes that could turn her to mush.

"If it would keep you here another day, I wouldn't mind if you'd given me the plague."

Two hours later they were back at the house. Abby followed Owen upstairs. Thank goodness he had listened to her because he felt even worse now than he had earlier.

Now he was dizzy, hot and cold at the same time and he felt as if he were watching the world go by from underwater. Nothing seemed quite real. It was the fever, Dr. Kayla Burns, the new physician in town, had explained. She'd given him a strong antibiotic and sent him home for bed rest. She said he had one of the worst cases of strep she'd seen in years.

Abby perched on the edge of the mattress and laid a wet washcloth on his forehead. He sighed audibly. It felt so good, the cold cloth on his hot skin, and Abby so close. He certainly wasn't pleased he was sick, but he was sure as hell glad she hadn't left. It just never occurred to him that she would get so upset about him being late. Had he known, he'd have called one of the guys to come over and tell her what was up.

"You took the antibiotic and the ibuprofen?"

"Uh-huh," he said without opening his eyes.

"Just sleep then. A couple of doses and you'll feel better."

She started to get up but he grabbed her hand. "Abby?"

"Yeah?"

"You going to be here when I wake up?"

"I'm going to be here."

An answer to his prayers. There was a God in heaven.

"You're not going today then?"

"Not today," she said. "Who would take care of you— Edgar?"

He smiled, his eyes still shut. "We'll talk when I get up."

"We don't have to talk." She pulled her cool hand from his.

He opened his eyes and caught her gaze. She was so

beautiful, so . . . Abby. "We *do* have to talk," he said firmly. "I have a question for you. One I'm ready to hear the answer to."

She blinked. He had obviously caught her by surprise. But it was a good surprise, he thought, hoped.

Her face softened as she reached down to stroke his cheek. Her cool hand felt good there too. "Sweet dreams."

It was late afternoon when Owen awoke. The digital clock beside the bed read 4:15. Had he really slept more than five hours? He got up to go to the bathroom and had just sat back on the edge of the bed when Abby stuck her head in the bedroom door. "I thought I heard you up. You OK?"

He lifted his head from his hands. "Peachy, darlin'."

She stepped through the doorway. The room-darkening shades were pulled so that the bedroom was shadowy on the August afternoon, but even in the false twilight he could make out the hesitant smile on her face, the warmth in her eyes. She was such a compassionate woman—she could have been a physician. But then Abby was the kind of person who could have been—could be—anything she wanted. Watching her here in the semi-darkness, he just knew she was going to write that book and sell it with many more to come.

"Want some tea?" she asked. "Or would you rather have something cold?"

He ran his hand down his throat. It felt constricted and it was hard to swallow. When he spoke, it smarted. "I think I'll have something cold, but you don't have to get it. I can do it myself."

She acted as if she were going to leave, then turned back. She came to the bedside and sat beside him. For a long moment they were silent. "I'm sorry I got so angry last night," she said.

He lifted his hand lamely. "No apology necessary. I had it coming. I was late for every dinner, every date, every party for two years." There. He'd admitted what he'd known all along and had been too thickheaded to face.

She flopped backward onto his bed that still smelled of her skin and their lovemaking. If she left him now, he doubted he'd ever wash the sheets again.

"I overreacted." She hesitated. "Because you do seem different. I should have realized something was wrong, rather than thinking you just hadn't bothered to show up."

"I made a lot of mistakes over a long period of time," he said thoughtfully. "I can't expect you to just forget it all as if it never happened."

She sighed. "I'm so confused, Owen. I was so sure of myself, of my choices the day I drove into Land's End. I had accepted the fact that you and I were going our separate ways, and now . . ." She lifted her hand into the air and let it fall over her forehead.

He lay back on the bed, his legs dangling beside hers. They stared at the ceiling fan together, watching it rotate. "Tell me why you left me," he said quietly.

"No. It's silly. Moot at this point. No need for whining and accusations."

He rolled onto his side, propping his head up with one hand. When she turned to look at him, they were almost nose-to-nose. "I need to hear it from you and you need to tell me, Abby."

She stared at the ceiling again, groaning aloud. "It sounds so ridiculous, worse than irreconcilable differences." She gestured.

"Say it anyway."

She took a breath. "You lost interest in me. In us."

His first impulse was to tell her that he had never stopped loving her. He hadn't lost interest in her; his attention had only temporarily been elsewhere. But he remained silent, letting her have her say.

"I swear, Owen, it would have hurt less if there had been another woman."

That smarted, but still he didn't speak. He listened, as he should have listened when they were still married, when he knew they were headed for troubled waters and she was trying to rescue them both.

"Work became everything to you. I was just an inconvenience, an annoyance. Every time I tried to talk to you about spending more time together, you put me off. You kept talking about sailing trips to Europe after you made your way up in that damned company." She looked at him. "I didn't want a trip to Europe, Owen, just a walk in the park with you."

He rolled onto his back, running his hand through his hair. This was hard to hear, but she was right. She was absolutely right. He had become obsessed at Jacob & Jacob. And he'd assumed she'd wanted the same things he'd wanted. He'd been too much of an idiot to realize he hadn't wanted those things either.

Not without Abby.

"I wanted so badly to quit my job and try writing full-time. I would have been willing to live in a smaller place, exchange fewer presents at Christmas. I could even have taken in editorial work."

Owen honestly couldn't remember Abby being unhappy at the publishing house in Boston, but then, honestly when he looked back, he couldn't remember much of anything about Abby's job. He'd never even been to her office.

She took a deep breath. "I know all of this seems like a silly reason to leave your husband. You didn't beat me, you didn't drink, and there was no other woman. You just didn't seem to love me anymore, maybe because you'd loved me for so many years." Her voice grew softer. "And I deserve to be loved, Owen," she said, her voice thick with emotion.

He let her words sink in before he spoke. He gave himself time to let the tightness in his chest ease. Her words hurt him, but not as much as it hurt to know how she had suffered.

Abby waited, but it was not an uncomfortable silence.

"I don't know what to say," he started slowly, "except that I'm sorry. All the things you said are true, except I never stopped loving you. My energies just became misdirected." He turned his head to look at her; she continued to stare at the ceiling fan. "I guess you'd been there for so many years, that I assumed you always would be."

"It was the same for me," she whispered. "I thought you'd always be there for me, and then you weren't. I learned the hard way not to take things for granted."

Again the room was silent, except for the whirl of the ceiling fan. This time the lump in Owen's throat wasn't caused by the strep virus. He slid his hand over the rumpled sheets to cover hers. "So, now what?" he asked.

"I don't know."

Owen slid his arm under her shoulders and she allowed him to draw her close to him. He felt lousy, as if he'd been beaten, but to hold Abby like this, did more for his morale than any antibiotic.

They lay there on the bed in silence for a long time, ten minutes, maybe fifteen. Eventually she sat up. "Hot tea or ginger ale?"

"Ginger ale."

"Anything else I can get you?"

"No." He was feeling a little dizzy so he slid over in the bed until his head rested on a pillow. "I need to call Zack and tell him I can't go by the Anderson house and take those measurements." Suddenly he sat up. "Oh, no."

She stopped in the doorway. "What?"

He tapped his forehead and gestured. "My team. The doctor said I'm contagious for three days. I have practice tomorrow and Wednesday. What am I going to do about practice?"

She lifted her shoulder in a shrug. "Cancel?"

He looked at her horrified. "Cancel practice? I can't do that." He put his hands together in a begging motion. "You'll have to run practice for me. Please?"

"Oh, no. I'm no coach. Get someone else."

"Who?"

"I don't know, Zack or Ben," she suggested.

"The enemy?" He feigned shock. "Besides, they have their own teams to coach."

"I am *not* coaching your softball team."

"You'll be fine. Better than fine," he argued. "You'll be great."

She turned in the doorway and headed down the hall. "No, Owen. Do you hear me? Absolutely not." Her voice grew no softer as she went down the stairs. Now she was yelling. "I am not, under any circumstances, taking over your coaching job in your absence!"

Fourteen

"All right, listen up, ladies," Abby addressed the team.

"Where's Coach Thomas?" Nell tossed a ball into her glove again and again.

"He's sick, so I'm substituting for him," Abby explained to the pint-size catcher. "Just until he's feeling better."

"Got the chicken pox?" Monica tugged on the pink tutu she always wore to practice over her shorts. "I had the chicken pox, and I had dots like freckles all over me and my mom bought me popsicles and I got to rent a whole bunch of movies from the video store."

"I had chicken pox, too," Tiffany chimed in.

Abby chuckled. "Ladies, ladies, Coach doesn't have chicken pox; he has something called strep throat." She stood in front of the team; they were lined up on the bench in the home dugout.

"Does he feel really bad?" Whitney asked.

Abby nodded. "He does, and he's contagious. That's why—"

"What's contagious?" Tonesha interrupted.

"It means you can catch it." Nell elbowed Tonesha.

Tonesha pushed her back.

Abby came between the two girls before they got into a tussle. "That's enough, Nell. Tonesha." She addressed the entire team. "It's time we got started. First a jog around the field to get warmed up and then we'll start our exercises. Let's go."

"You're going to run, too?" Nell popped up off the bench.

"Sure. Bet I can beat you!" Abby took off around the infield and the thirteen girls followed her like goslings queued up behind Mother Goose.

"You think we ought to hire one of those intervention organizations?"

Owen slowly woke from his nap, thinking he heard Ben and Zack talking. But how could that be? He was at home, sick in bed. He had to be dreaming.

"Intervention?" Zack questioned seriously.

"Yeah, you know, those companies that will kidnap your loved ones from cults for the price of two mortgages, and then deprogram them in seedy motel rooms."

"I know this is serious, Ben, but I don't think Abby is running a cult."

Owen tried to drag himself from the depths of sleep, groggy and confused, but not so confused that he didn't want to know what was going on. For a dream, Zack and Ben sounded awfully real. He forced his eyes open and tried to focus.

Sure enough, there they were. Curly and Mo, as Abby called them. Ben stood over the bed, staring at Owen. Zack stood behind him.

"It's not just for cults," Ben said. "Addictions, too. For instance, if your brother is hooked on cocaine, they hold him long enough to bring him back to earth and convince him to check into detox."

This was no dream. The whirling ceiling fan over the bed was dusty and dreams never had dusty furniture.

"You think Abby qualifies as an addiction?" Zack asked.

"If she isn't, buddy, I don't know what is." Ben pointed at Owen. "Look at him!"

Owen squinted in the bright light. The fools had turned on his bedroom lights. "What are you guys doing here?" He grabbed a pillow and pulled it over his face. It smelled of Abby and he couldn't resist inhaling deeply.

"We're here to rescue you, man." Zack pulled the pillow off his head. "Come quietly and we won't tie you up and take you to a seedy motel and I won't have to mortgage my house."

"What the hell are you talking about and why are you in my bedroom in the middle of the day?" Owen sat up and scratched his bare belly. He'd been sleeping in nothing but a pair of boxers because he'd been so hot, even with the air turned up.

Ben sat on the edge of the bed. "She's still here." He sounded as if he was signing Owen's death warrant, that or reading his will.

"Yes, Abby's still here."

"Why?" Ben opened his arms. "She's all better. Cured. She was supposed to be on her way."

"I'm sick." Owen hugged the pillow and gave Ben a none-too-gentle nudge with his foot. "So, get out. Go home. Aren't you two supposed to be employed?"

"I got your message about being sick yesterday, but Savannah had checked the answering machine for me and forgot to tell me you had called," Zack said. "I came as soon as I heard."

"And brought Nutso with you." He pushed Ben with his bare foot again.

Ben stood. "I'm just trying to protect you." He raised his hands as if to surrender. "We thought you might be in trouble."

"Well, I'm not. I have strep throat and Abby stayed to coach my team until I'm not contagious anymore." Owen didn't dare tell them that Abby had initially stayed to take care of him. He didn't want to hear Zack and Ben's comments on that one.

"You're letting her coach?" Zack asked with surprise. "A woman?"

"Well, they are little girls." Owen frowned. "Besides, Abby knows a lot about softball. She played in college. She was a mean first baseman."

Ben shook his head, pacing beside the bed. "She stops by to pick up some stuff and now she's been here more than a week. It doesn't sound good, Owen." He shook his head. "Doesn't sound good at all. Not for Bachelors, Inc. and not for Owen Thomas."

"What do I have to say to make you two understand that I want Abby to be here? Hell, I'd marry her again this minute if she'd have me."

Everyone was silent. His buddies stared at him with shock.

Ben turned to Zack. "He's not kidding; he really is sick. Delirious with fever."

It was enough to break the tension between them.

Owen flung the pillow and hit both of them with the one blow. They laughed and Zack picked it up and tossed it back onto the bed.

"Look, I know you guys don't understand. I know this is really weird for you, Abby being my ex-wife." He lowered his voice. "But I love her." He paused. "And I think maybe she still loves me. And if there's any way I can convince her to stay here, I will. You guys might as well know that up front."

"What about Bachelors, Inc.? The GAG Club?" Ben asked.

Owen met his gaze. "The hell with it."

Zack sighed. "Look, we're not trying to interfere in your life. We just want you to be happy."

"Abby makes me happy," Owen said firmly.

For a moment, all three were quiet. Again, it was Ben who spoke up first. Owen could tell that he wasn't convinced Abby was in Owen's best interest, but at least he knew when to back down.

"Well, we just came by to see if you needed anything. Chicken soup, a beer?"

"Mom sent over chicken noodle soup yesterday and I couldn't swallow a beer right now if I tried."

Ben hooked his thumbs into his jean pockets. "So, you want us to go?"

"You don't need intervention?" Zack teased.

Owen grinned. "No intervention."

After the warm-up exercises, Abby worked on base-running skills, had the girls play a game of catch, and then let them scrimmage. The practice went well and she was pleased not only with the girls' progress but with her own ability to teach them. She couldn't wait to get home and tell Owen how it went.

It had never occurred to Abby that she might like coaching a girls' softball team, but after today, she wondered if maybe she should volunteer, too. Surely Myrtle Beach must have softball. Driving back to Owen's, she actually found herself looking forward to Wednesday's practice.

She guessed that meant she was staying at least until Wednesday. The question was, then what? Owen obviously didn't want her to go. And a part of her didn't want to go either. Talking yesterday about why she had left him had been good for them both.

Even with Owen feeling bad, they had enjoyed the rest of the day together and this morning he had felt well enough to have breakfast with her. She had worked on her book for several hours, and now after softball practice she felt that she'd had a very productive day. She liked Land's End, she liked the people and it seemed like the perfect place to write. Life moved slower here than in Boston and that was exactly what she'd been looking for when she'd taken Jess's cottage for the year.

Abby turned into the driveway and spotted both Zack's and Ben's cars. "Great," she muttered.

She had half a mind to pull right around the circular drive and go up to the corner to wait until they left. But she didn't. She had a right to be here. Owen wanted her here and it was none of their business.

Edgar met her inside the door. "Hey, boy. How's my big boy?" She lingered long enough to run a hand over the dog's glossy black and brown coat. Edgar wagged his tail greedily.

Abby strode up the stairs. "Do you think we need quarantine signs to keep out the riffraff?" she said, as she walked into Owen's bedroom.

Sure enough, Zack and Ben were there.

"Abby! How'd it go?" Owen brightened the moment he saw her.

"Good." She nodded. "Great. I'll tell you all about it when these two are gone." She hooked her thumb in Zack's and Ben's direction, wondering how Owen could look so sexy, lying in bed in ladybug boxers, his face red with fever. "I wouldn't want to give away any of our secrets."

"We can take a hint." Ben put up his hands. "We're going."

"No, they can't take a hint," Owen said. "I told them to leave five minutes ago."

Abby started out of the bedroom. "Stay as long as you want, guys; you're already infected. I'm going for a run." She waved over her shoulder. "Back after a bit, Owen."

He waved. "I'll be waiting."

She halted just outside the door and stuck her head in. She was so glad she and Owen had talked last night. She felt much better about herself and her overreaction to his being late. She felt better about *them*. The word *hopeful* popped up in her head.

"And Owen—"

She liked this light banter between her and Owen. It made her feel the way she had when they'd first started dating. There was that chemical excitement between them, the kind you could feel, the kind you could smell on the air.

"Yeah?"

"Nice boxers."

Zack and Ben burst into raucous laughter, their voices still echoing as Abby went down the stairs.

Abby passed Owen's parents' house as she headed back up the street after her run. Lillian was headed across the backyard toward Owen's back door carrying a plastic butter dish filled with something. Edgar was hot on her heels.

Abby cut across the lawn. "Hi, Lillian."

She halted, holding the large butter dish out of reach of Edgar's eager nose. "You're still here, I see." She raised one perfectly plucked eyebrow.

Abby grinned. She really didn't mind Lillian's little comments; she just accepted the woman for who she was. "Still here."

Lillian shook her head. "Maurice says it's none of my business, but I hope you two aren't making a big mistake."

Abby scratched Edgar behind the ears. She didn't know what was in the dish Lillian held, but the dog was certainly interested. More chicken soup, no doubt. "Is that right?" she said, noncommittal. She was not getting into a discussion with Lillian in the middle of the backyard about her and Owen's relationship.

Lillian continued to shake her perfectly combed head. "The divorce was so hard on Owen, and I'm sure on you, too, dear," she quickly added with her southern charm. "I would hate for him to go through all that again."

Abby didn't know what to say, but she felt as if she needed to defend Owen. After all, it was his life and he was an intelligent man. He could make his own choices, his own decisions. "We've been talking a lot," she said carefully. "I think we realize now that we both made some mistakes."

Lillian eyed Abby in her running shorts and tank top. "So, do you have plans as to when you'll be headed for Myrtle Beach?" She smiled thinly. "I know you're anxious to get started on that novel of yours."

"Actually, I've started the book," Abby answered proudly. "It's going pretty well."

Lillian lowered the butter dish to her hip, still keeping it out of Edgar's reach. "I admire your tenacity," she said, and she sounded sincere. "Most women I know gave up their dreams of professional success to have children and provide a home for their husbands. Certainly, they have their little jobs." She fluttered her free hand. "But they were never able to reach for what they truly wanted."

Abby twisted the ball of her foot in the grass. "I'd still like to have children." She glanced up. "Don't you think women can have a successful career and a family?"

Lillian knitted her brows. "Perhaps some women. Someone like you. I honestly think you could do anything you wanted." She sighed. "Of course, I always thought that was part of the reason for the breakup. That you wanted children and Owen didn't."

"No." Abby shook her head, surprised by Lillian's comment. She had secretly had the same fear, but she and Owen had never reached the point of seriously discussing being parents. "He never said he didn't want children."

"Well, I'm sure I just misunderstood. You know how it is with mothers and sons." She offered the plastic container to Abby. "Soup for Owen. Would you mind? I'm awfully susceptible to strep."

"Not at all." Abby forced a smile and accepted the soup. The woman was such an enigma, offering compliments one moment, caustic remarks the next.

"Tell him I hope he's feeling better. I don't want to call and wake him."

Abby forced another smile. "I'll tell him." With a wave, she crossed the lawn and went in the back door. Zack and Ben were leaving out the front door.

"Later." Zack gave a wave.

"Take care of him," Ben called.

She waved.

Putting the chicken soup in the fridge with yesterday's, Abby went upstairs to shower. Once she had changed into clean clothes, she stuck her head in Owen's doorway. "Hey."

"Hey."

She ran a hand towel over her wet hair.

"Have a good run?"

"Great."

He patted the edge of the bed. He lay stretched out on top of the comforter, still wearing nothing but those cute ladybug boxers.

She sat down. "Your mom sent over more chicken noodle soup."

"Oh, good. As if I can't open a can on my own." He tucked his hands behind his head.

"Exactly my thought." She wrinkled her nose. "But it was easier to take the Campbell's than to argue with her."

He took her hand in his. "You going to work for a while?"

"I was thinking about it. It's really going well, Owen." She met his gaze. "I'm so excited."

"I'm excited for you." He turned her hand in his. "So, tell me how practice went."

She tossed the damp towel on the end of the bed and slid in. She settled her head on the pillow beside his. "I think they could beat Ben's boys, or at least give them a good run for their money. Girls play differently than boys, but this group—their hearts are really in it."

"Ben wants to play next Saturday. Kind of an exhibition game to start the season." He glanced sideways at her. "What would you think about staying another week and being my assistant coach—just for that game?" he added quickly.

She sighed. She still didn't know what the right thing to do was. Owen had asked her to stay, but he hadn't said for what. To what end? Did he think that marriage could be in their future? She wasn't ready to ask him yet. Not ready to be that hopeful.

She fiddled with the hem of his ladybug boxers. "I seem to be making out fine on the laptop."

"And if you stayed, we could take that sailing trip we'd planned. This time, I'll pack dinner," he bribed.

She smiled slyly. "I think I can be persuaded to stay. Of course that will piss off Zack, Ben, Jess, and your mother. They were hoping I would be on my way sooner rather than later."

Owen chuckled. "Do we care what they think?"

She turned her head to face him, smiling. "Nope."

"Nope," he repeated.

Then he kissed her and that bud of hope inside her began to swell.

Fifteen

Abby dragged her hand through the water, watching it part and ripple around and over her fingers. The bay was a breathtaking blue-green beneath the sailboat, the sky a painted canvas of cloudless blue overhead. The sun shining brightly made it a magical August day.

"So, what do you think?" Owen sat aft on the deck, his knees drawn up to his chest, his hand on the rudder. The wind ruffled his short hair. He looked suntanned and relaxed, younger than he had in years. Land's End really was good for him.

Or was it her?

Abby turned her face into the wind. The salt spray was refreshing. "I love it!"

"The bay or the boat?" He grinned.

"All of it." She met his gaze. "You."

Keeping one hand on the rudder, he slid forward a little on the slick fiberglass deck and covered her hand with his. "I'm glad you stayed. I mean it."

"Me, too." She suddenly felt shy and glanced away. She was afraid this was too good to be true.

They had had a great week together. Within two days

of Owen's visit to the ER, he had been feeling better. They had spent the week working, practicing with the team, and getting to know each other again.

They had had few interruptions—not many calls or visits. Ben and Zack were staying away, though Abby didn't know if that was because Owen had asked them to, or they were just avoiding the situation. She liked to think they were giving him space to decide for himself what he wanted. What was best for him, not necessarily them and their little club. Either way, it had given them time alone. time to think and talk.

Today Abby felt happier than she'd been in years.

"So, how do you think the team will do tomorrow?" she asked, gazing out at the horizon.

"I don't know." He shook his head. "Ben's got some big kids, but agreed to stick with coach-pitch so we don't have to worry about that." He thought for a moment. "I think you're right. We ought to at least be able to hold our own."

"I think we'll do better than that." She grinned. "I think we're going to beat their tails."

"Either way, I appreciate your staying to help me out I'm just not cut out to deal with kids."

She thought about her desire to be a mother and what Lillian had said the other day. "What makes you say that Don't you like children?"

"Certainly I like children." He sat up on his knees and brought the sailboat around. "With a little salt and pepper maybe a dash of garlic powder."

She laughed and gave him a push, but somewhere inside she gave a little sigh of disappointment. She certainly thought she could live a productive life without being a parent, but old dreams died hard sometimes. She considered questioning Owen further on his thoughts on children, on his thoughts of *them* having children. Why didn't he want to be a father? Why hadn't he ever come right out and told her? How could his mother know something important like this and she not?

But in the end, Abby decided against talking about it. They had dredged up so much in the last two weeks. They'd shared so much of themselves, and she knew that was hard for Owen. There would be time later for such discussions. And who knew? Her biological clock wasn't ticking too loudly yet. Maybe Owen would change his mind with time. Besides, she was getting way ahead of herself. He hadn't actually asked her to marry him again yet.

"Look there." Owen pointed.

A tiny island came into view as the boat skimmed over the water. "Is that the island you were telling me about?"

He guided them into shallower water. "It's not very big, but it's shaded and there aren't any mosquitoes. I thought it would be the perfect place for a picnic."

She rose on her knees as they glided toward the sandy shore. "Does it have a name?"

"Mm hmm."

She glanced back at him from the bow.

"Abby Island."

She laughed, but she was touched. This romantic side of him seemed stronger than she remembered. She liked it. Maybe it was just something that came with wisdom and time.

"Want me to drop anchor?"

"Nah. You don't have to get wet." He lowered the mainsail. It flapped in the wind and died as it settled against the mast. "I'll jump out and tow us to shore."

She pulled her T-shirt over her head. "I wore my bathing suit. I don't mind."

He eyed her bikini top. "Can't say I mind either."

Laughing, she tossed the anchor and it quickly caught on the sandy bottom. They were in less than four feet of water. Grasping the mast, she stood up. The boat rocked slightly, but she caught her balance and stepped out of her shorts. "I was thinking about a dip before dinner."

She gazed out, a naughty thought popping up in her head. They had sailed into a cove of the bay. Maybe it had even once been a river. For as far as she could see, they were alone. Before she gave herself time to reconsider, she reached back and unhooked her bikini top.

When Owen turned back from securing the rudder, his mouth dropped open.

Flushing with pleasure, she dropped her red bikini bottom on the deck and jumped in.

"Wait for me!" he hollered.

Laughing, she swam away from the boat. The water was surprisingly clear and warm and felt delicious on her bare skin. A school of tiny fish swam by and Abby reached out to try to scoop one in her hand.

She heard a splash and turned to see Owen behind her. He had shed his shirt, but she couldn't tell if he was wearing trunks or not. She guessed not.

She floated on her back, paddling with her hands.

"I can't believe you did that." Owen was grinning ear to ear as he swam up to her.

"What?"

"That." He pointed to her bare breasts.

"Why not?"

"I don't know." He ran his hand down her arm. "I just don't see you as an impulsive person."

"But you like a little impulsiveness?" She felt warm all over now. Having Owen stare like this was an incredibly exhilarating experience.

"I like surprises." He leaned over and kissed her on the mouth. "Especially delicious ones like this."

She licked her salty lips and paddled around him. "I just thought I could use a little sun. You know all the women go topless in Myrtle Beach."

"They do not." He splashed her.

She stood up and her toes sank into the silty bottom. She splashed him back. "On the private beach I'll be on, they do."

He waded up to her. Her pale breasts bobbed up and down between them. "I was really hoping you'd decide to stay here in Land's End with me."

Her gaze met his. "And then what?"

She was thrilled that he didn't look away.

"I was thinking of a serious second chance."

She moved closer and he rested his hands on her hips under the water. "Meaning?"

"Meaning I want to marry you," he said softly. "Again. And this time I'll do it right. I'll be the husband you deserve. I'll love you and treasure you the way I should have to begin with."

She smoothed the wet hair on his chest with her palm. "I suppose I should be asking you since I was the one who left."

He brushed her cheek with the back of his hand. "We could ask each other." He grinned boyishly.

196   *Colleen Faulkner*

"OK."

"One, two, three," he said.

"Will you marry me?" they said in unison.

"Abby?"

"Owen?"

They both laughed and their voices echoed overhead
mingling with the sounds of the seagulls.

"You think this makes any sense whatsoever?" she
asked.

He drew her closer, enveloping her in his arms. He was
definitely not wearing a swimsuit.

"Does anything on this earth make sense to you? Be
cause it doesn't to me."

She laughed. "The guys are really going to be upset
with you. As a married man, you would no longer qualify
as a member. You're going to be ousted from Bachelors
Inc."

"They can't kick me out." He brushed his lips against
hers in a tantalizingly slow motion. "I'm a copresident.
own stock."

She laughed as she ran her fingers through his hair. It
was damp with salt air and curled around her fingers.
"How many people do you think can claim they've been
proposed to while totally naked?"

He touched her nose with the tip of his playfully. "Prob
ably more than you think."

She laughed and hugged him. He kissed her bare shoul
der. "You know, it's these cute freckles that got me in the
first place," he murmured.

She pulled back a little to look at him. The water swirled
around them. "My freckles?"

"Yup. That summer I moved to Land's End, you were always wearing those sexy tank tops."

"I was ten. Ten-year-olds can't be sexy."

"But I was ten, too. I couldn't keep my eyes off your freckles. The guys were dreaming of playing professional baseball and I was dreaming about little girls with freckled shoulders."

She couldn't stop smiling. "I love you, Owen Thomas."

"I love you, Abby Thomas."

She traced the cleft in his chin with a wet fingertip. "You know, the judge gave me back my own name when we divorced. So, I'm really Abby Maconnal again."

"But I never took my name away," he breathed against her lips. "I never resigned myself to the divorce because I never lost hope."

She molded her hips to his, feeling pulses of excitement as he stroked her bare buttocks underwater. "Think we should go ashore or try it here in the water?"

"Ladies' choice."

She grabbed his shoulders and drew her legs up and around his waist. In the water, it was easy for him to hold her up. "I'm thinking both," she whispered huskily in his ear.

Owen threw back his head and laughed. "My thoughts exactly."

Abby paced nervously back and forth, her scorebook clutched in her arms. She pulled her Red Sox ball cap off, wiped the sweat from her brow and replaced the cap. It was a hot day and the humidity was high. The sun was so bright that she squinted, even in sunglasses.

Owen was still running infield practice. He was hitting grounders to the girls and they were throwing them back to one of the mothers. In the outfield, a father threw pop flies to the outfielders.

Ben had agreed they would use a softball rather than a baseball; his team was already lined up on the bench, listening to their coach's last instructions.

"So, how do you think they'll fare?"

Abby turned around to see Max at the dugout gate. As always, he had a date beside him. This woman, in her mid-sixties, wore her red hair tied back in a ponytail and a Baltimore Orioles tee shirt. She was eating peanuts.

"I think they'll do great," Abby answered with more enthusiasm than she felt.

"Let me introduce you to my friend. This is Myrna. Myrna loves baseball."

Myrna offered her hand and Abby shook it. "All sports," the redhead said. "I never miss an O's game on TV. Tape 'em when I'm not home or they play late on the West Coast."

"Well, I'm not sure this game will be as exciting as watching the Orioles play," Abby said. "But it was nice of you to come."

"Here comes the umpire." Max indicated the man dressed in blue, carrying a facemask. "Guess we'd better find a good seat on the bleachers."

"Thanks for coming by." Abby smiled.

"Wouldn't miss it for the world." Max gave her a pat on the back and then led Myrna away.

"All right, let's hit the dugout," Owen hollered to the team. "I want to see good throws, and then you can run in."

One by one, the infielders followed Owen's instructions and filed into the dugout. The outfielders were right behind them. All the girls were chattering with nervous excitement. Owen looked plain nervous.

"Come on," Abby whispered in his ear. "Smile. This is supposed to be fun."

"It will be fun after it's over," he whispered back.

She elbowed him and then turned to the bench. "Listen up, ladies. The announcer will call your name, you'll run to first, then up the line to home base, just like we practiced. Once we've sung the national anthem we play ball. Any questions?"

Whitney's hand shot up. "Can I go to the bathroom?"

Owen nodded and Whitney took off.

Kari's hand went up. "Can we chew green bubble gum? Tonesha says we can only chew pink, but I don't like pink."

"Ladies, ladies, we need to be concentrating on the game here." Owen glanced nervously toward the visitors' side dugout. Ben's boys, the Astros, were lined up on the bench, looking way too serious. "Remember, this is a thinking game."

"When the game's over, do we really get ice cream? Coach Abby says we get ice cream," Tiffany wound one of her braids around her finger. "I'm lactose intolerant, you know. I have to have my pills if I'm going to have ice cream."

"First we play," Abby said, tapping Tiffany on the brim of her hat. "Then ice cream."

The announcer spoke over the intercom and Owen clapped his hands together. "This is it, ladies. Now remember, I don't care if we win or lose, just as long as you play your best. Let's go." He walked to the dugout gate. "Listen up for your names."

They moved quickly through the opening ceremonies and the first pitch was thrown. At first, Abby was so nervous she could barely watch. Truthfully, she was nervous for Owen. She knew he was afraid the Red Sox were going to get creamed. The girls seemed to have none of the concentration that the boys had. And yet, as they reached the bottom of the first inning at 0-1, the girls began to fall into a rhythm. Somehow they could talk about green sparkle nailpolish and still beat a runner home.

At the end of the first inning the girls were ahead of the boys by one run. And the boys didn't like it one bit.

In the second inning the boys scored two more runs. The girls only scored one. It was tied up. In the third inning the boys scored another run, and then Nell hit a home run.

Ben cut behind home plate with a substitute list. "All right," he muttered to Abby as he handed her a tiny sheet of paper. "Now we're bringing in the big guns." He seemed amused.

Abby laughed. "You guys take this stuff entirely too seriously," she told him as he walked away. "Maybe you boys ought to loosen up a little like our girls."

By the fourth inning the game was once again tied up when Ben's best hitter knocked a ball to the fence. Luckily he was the only one on base.

"This is making me crazy," Owen said as he snatched off his cap and ran his fingers through his hair. Abby heard the bat crack against the ball and glanced up. One of the boys hit a line drive. Tonesha, on second base, lifted her glove, but a second too late. Even before the ball hit her, Abby saw Owen take off across the infield.

"Tonesha!" he shouted.

Sixteen

"Tonesha!" Abby ran after Owen.

Owen reached the little girl first, went down on one knee, and lifted her gently into his arms. "Tonesha, honey, can you hear me?" he asked gently.

Abby could hear the terror in his voice, though he appeared dead calm.

The little girl's eyes were shut, but as Owen called her name, her lids fluttered.

"That's it, sweetie, open your eyes." Owen brushed the hair from her face. A purple egg-shaped lump was already rising on her forehead.

Tonesha's lids lifted and she looked up into Owen's eyes. A crowd had formed around them—the umpire, all the players. Tonesha's parents came running across the infield.

Tonesha blinked. "Coach?"

Owen smiled with obvious relief. "Hey, sweetie. You feeling OK?"

She blinked again, then focused on him with big brown eyes. "I can't believe I missed that dag-goned ball! It was coming right at me!"

Owen glanced over his shoulder at Abby and gave her a shaky smile. She could tell by the look on his face that the little girl was going to be all right.

"Okay, ladies, gentlemen," Abby clapped her hands together, taking control of the gathering crowd. "Let's get back to our positions. Give Tonesha some room to breathe."

As Abby urged the players away from their teammate, Owen went through a few simple mental tests with Tonesha, keeping the little girl seated on the ground. When her parents, the umpire, and Owen agreed that she seemed to be all right, they let her get to her feet.

Tonesha seemed embarrassed as she jumped up and snatched her dusty hat off the ground. "Someone have my glove?"

The parents from both sides got to their feet on the bleachers and clapped for Tonesha. She grinned shyly as she walked off the field with Owen and her parents.

"I don't understand why I have to go to the hospital," Tonesha complained.

"Just for a quick check," her mother, flushed with relief, told her.

Tonesha glanced up at Owen. "Do I have to, Coach?"

Owen grimaced. "Afraid so, sweetie. But why don't you meet us at the ice cream shop afterward?"

Tonesha turned to her father. "Can we, Dad?"

The man grinned, lowering his arm over his daughter's shoulder. "I think that could be arranged."

With Tonesha taken care of, Owen sent another player in for second base and the game began again.

"You OK?" Abby asked Owen as the batter stepped up to the plate.

"Yeah, I'm fine. I'm just glad she's OK." He adjusted his ball cap. "She scared the pants off me. Can you imagine how scared her parents must have been?" He shook his head. "I don't think I could take it."

She glanced at him. They really did need to talk about children. She needed to get that settled between them. "But you handled the whole situation great." She brushed her hand against his arm. "I was proud of you, Owen."

They exchanged a look that made her warm to her toes. Then Owen turned back to the game. "Let's look lively, girls!"

Abby tucked the score book under her arm and clapped her hands. "All right, let's go, ladies. One more out and you're up!"

The game moved more quickly from there on. Before Abby knew it, it was the bottom of the sixth and last inning. The boys had seven runs, the girls six. Abby had bitten her nails to the quick. She watched as Owen pitched to Whitney. The little girl was perfectly relaxed. She even stepped out of the batter's box between balls to wave to a friend in the bleachers.

Owen looked as if he wanted to throw up.

Whitney hit a single. Monica struck out and returned to the dugout to put her tutu back on. The umpire did not allow tutus on the ball field. Kari hit a single, but Whitney was called out sliding into home.

The Astros were ahead, seven to six. The girls had two outs, a runner on second. Nell stepped up to bat.

"Come on, Nell!" Abby called from the dugout.

"Hit it!" Kari shouted from behind the dugout fence. "Knock it down their throats!"

Abby turned to Kari in surprise, wondering if she ought to suggest she tone it down a bit. The little girl smiled sweetly. Nell missed two nice pitches, then held back on three balls in a row. Abby could see from where she stood that Owen was so nervous he could barely toss the ball over the plate.

Abby heard the crack of the bat against the ball, broke into a grin, and leaped in the air, trying to hold her score book and clap at the same time. Before the little girl reached first base, Abby knew the ball was headed for the fence. The fans on the bleachers jumped up, clapping and hollering.

Nell rounded second as the ball hit the ground and rolled toward the fence. Two outfielders went after it. Ben shouted for them to throw it to home. The base coach on third waved Nell by.

"Go! Go!" the girls in the dugout screamed. Kari scored. A boy in the outfield threw the ball to the short-stop, who whipped around and hurled it toward home plate. The masked catcher leaped into the air as Nell slid for home plate.

Abby thought her heart would leap out of her chest.

Nell slid across the plate, slamming into the catcher. She looked up at the umpire hovering over her.

"Safe!" the umpire boomed, slicing the air with both hands.

The girls in the dugout screamed and burst from the dugout fence, running across the field to home plate. Grinning, Owen walked toward Nell as she picked herself up off the ground.

Abby flashed a smile at Owen. He gave her a thumbs-up and she laughed. Life was good.

* * *

"I still can't believe your girls beat my boys," Ben said good-naturedly. "Pass another slab of pepperoni."

After buying ice cream for the girls, and sending them home with their parents, Abby and Owen had joined Ben, Zack and Savannah for dinner at the Pizza Palace.

"Don't feel too badly," Owen winked at Abby and dropped a piece of pizza onto Ben's paper plate. He was so relieved that the game was over, so relieved that Tonesha was all right. "It was really all in the coaching."

"It was not!" Abby elbowed Owen. "Those girls are good ballplayers and you know it." She glanced up at Ben across the table. "And now you know it, too."

"That Nell, she's something," Savannah said through a mouthful of pizza. "She goes to my school and we always try to get her on our team when we play on the playground."

"I've got to hand it to you, Buddy." Ben wiped his mouth with a napkin. "I didn't think you—*they*—could do it, but they did." He grinned at Owen across the table. "Congratulations."

Owen leaned back in his chair, resting his arm on the back of Abby's. It felt so good to have her at his side. He was so excited at the prospect of being married to her again, having her in his bed again and hearing her laugh every night and every morning. "I'm just glad it's over. I'll really be glad when the season is over."

"How can you say that?" Zack refilled his daughter's glass. "You're a natural."

"The girls love you," Abby said.

Owen rubbed her back. "I suppose it is fun. I like seeing them improve their game."

"I like seeing Owen coach players in dance skirts myself," Zack said over the rim of his glass.

"I can't believe I'm taking all this abuse." Owen opened his arms, not really minding it a bit. "Maybe we should change the subject."

Abby eyed him.

Owen knew that she knew what he was going to say next. He hadn't told Zack and Ben that he and Abby were going to give their relationship another try. They didn't know that one of the bachelors of Bachelors, Inc. was about to give up his status to become a married man again. He suspected Abby had assumed he wanted to tell them by himself, but Owen wanted her there. After all, it was a mutual decision.

She wrinkled her nose. "Do you think this is a good idea?"

He slipped his hand under the table to take hers in reassurance. "Why not? I'm happy. I want my friends to know how happy I am."

"Wait a minute. What's going on here?" Ben's gaze narrowed suspiciously.

"I told you," Zack muttered under his breath. "Didn't I tell you this was coming?"

Owen gave Abby's hand a squeeze. He could tell she was nervous. She thought the guys didn't like her, or at least didn't like her with him. But Owen knew that in the end, Zack and Ben would respect his decision and support him. In the end, no matter how hard a time they gave him, they always did.

"In case you guys haven't noticed," Owen said slowly,

"things have been going pretty well between Abby and me."

Ben rocked back in his chair, tucked his arms behind his head and stared at the ceiling.

"So well . . ." Owen took a deep breath, ". . . that I've asked Abby to marry me."

"You're going to get married?" Savannah perked up with interest. Then she frowned. "But didn't you used to be married and then you got a divorce like my mom and dad?"

"That's right." Abby leaned forward on the table. "But sometimes people make mistakes. Sometimes they get divorced when they shouldn't have."

Zack gave his daughter a hug. "Abby's right. Sometimes moms and dads need to get a divorce like me and Mom, but sometimes they don't."

"Like Uncle Owen and Abby?"

Owen flashed Zack a look of apology. He hadn't thought about Zack's situation. Zack and his wife were most definitely remaining divorced. His marriage had been a disaster from day one.

"It's OK, buddy," Zack said softly, meeting Owen's gaze. "We discuss this at least once a week."

Ben leaned forward on the table and folded his hands. He looked from Abby to Owen. "So, you want to give it another whirl, do you?"

"I love her, Ben," Owen said simply, not knowing any better reason to give him.

Abby looked at Owen, then at Ben and Zack. "I love him, guys. Sorry."

Both Zack and Ben were quiet for so long that Owen began to clench his jaw. Finally, Ben spoke up. "You sure

this is what you want? And I don't just mean you, Owen."
He cocked his head toward Owen, then addressed Abby.
"We always knew he was nuts. You were the one, Abby,
who had all the brains and the beauty."

She laughed.

"It's what we want," Owen said solemnly. "And I'm
counting on you guys to be here for me. I screwed up big
time being a husband once. I don't want to do it again. I
can't."

Zack stood and offered his big hand across the table.
"I guess congratulations are in order."

They shook and Owen felt waves of relief wash over
him. No matter what the guys thought, he knew he
wouldn't feel differently about Abby, but having their support would really help, not only because of their friendship
but the business they shared as well.

"I'm not shaking your hand," Zack said to Abby, coming around the table.

Abby rose to hug him.

Ben shook Owen's hand over half a pepperoni and
mushroom pizza. "Congrats, buddy. We didn't mean to
be a pain in the ass. You know we just want to see that
sunny smile of yours."

Owen knew that beneath the smart remark, Ben was
expressing his true feelings. "So, when's the big day?"
Ben rose from his chair to hug Abby, lifting her off her
feet. He gave her a big kiss on the lips.

"Hey, watch out," Owen hollered. "Those lips were
meant only for these."

Abby patted Ben's chest and came back to sit beside
Owen. She was smiling.

"Well, we haven't really discussed a date yet." Owen

poured Abby another soda. "She's got a book to write, you know."

Zack gave Savannah several coins and let the little girl walk over to the video games on the far side of the room.

Abby waited until Savannah was out of earshot. "We thought we'd give the present situation a few months." She sipped her drink. "Live in sin awhile."

The men laughed and Owen slipped his arm around Abby's shoulders again. He just couldn't believe his good luck. He couldn't believe he was getting a second chance. The one thing he knew was that this time, he was going to make sure he and Abby lived happily ever after. Whatever would make her happy, would make him happy. Abby could name it and if it was in his power, it was hers. That was the way he had always felt, only this time he would be sure he was always there to tell her so.

Owen rested his hand on the back of Abby's chair and brushed a kiss across her temple. "Love you," he murmured.

"Love you back."

Five days later Abby stood in the middle of the bathroom staring at her birth control pill pack. Thursday? Today was Thursday? This was impossible. Unbelievable.

"Is today Thursday?" she asked Edgar who sat in the doorway staring at her.

He made a chuffing sound. Definitely affirmative. The dog seemed to know what day it was, even if she was confused.

But Abby wasn't confused. She knew what day it was.

It was definitely Thursday. She had been in Land's End two and a half weeks, almost three.

She stared at the pill pack again. But this couldn't be.

She had taken every pill, even taking them at the same time of day, every day, as recommended. She had taken the twenty-one days of pink pills, then started the seven days of white on Sunday. She had taken them just as the doctor prescribed, just as she'd been taking them for years. But today was Thursday. She should have started her period Tuesday, yesterday at the latest.

Abby caught a glimpse of herself in the mirror. She was pasty white. Never in all these years of taking her pills had she ever been late. Not once. That wasn't how it worked.

She was pregnant.

Abby lowered the toilet lid and sat down, feeling dizzy. She couldn't stop staring at the pill pack, which was totally, unreasonably, ridiculous.

She felt numb from head to toe. "No, no," she murmured. "It's not possible."

The birth control pill, when taken properly, was ninety-eight percent effective. She knew that fact from the literature that came with every pill pack. She and her physician had discussed it when she'd first started taking them. Ninety-eight percent effective. That was nearly perfect.

No. A drug that was ninety-eight percent effective against pregnancy was a drug that was not effective two percent of the time. Abby was certain she had just become part of that two-percent minority.

"All right, calm down," she said aloud. It was OK to talk to herself because Owen was away for the day. H had gone to the McClusky house with the guys to talk with the homeowners and then out to another site. She had the day alone in the house to write. Or to fall apart . . .

"I have to stay calm and go get a home test," she said, rising off the seat.

Edgar chuffed. Again, he seemed to be in agreement.

"There's no need to panic." She dropped the pill pack into the trash can beside the sink and went down the hall. "There's no need to panic until the test comes up positive." She waved her hands trying to consciously slow her heartbeat and keep from hyperventilating. "No need to panic, Abby," she repeated.

Seventeen

Abby stared at the pregnancy test urine stick she held in her hand. It was blue. Definitely blue.

She glanced at her reflection in the bathroom mirror. "OK," she said aloud, watching the color drain from her face. "Now you can panic."

Pregnant.

On birth control pills and pregnant. The stuff single women's nightmares were made of.

Tears filled her eyes as she lowered herself onto the toilet lid. All those years she had wanted a baby and *now* she was pregnant. It couldn't have happened at a worse time. She gripped her stomach, feeling nauseous. Was it morning sickness or the cold slap of reality?

She wiped at her eyes with the back of her hand. She would need to make an appointment with a doctor, of course. Confirm her pregnancy with a blood test. But she knew was pregnant. She knew it.

So, now what?

Her heart pounded in her chest. Her mouth was dry, but her hands were sweaty.

Owen wanted her, but he didn't want children. Or at

least she didn't think he did. God, why hadn't she talked about this with him? It had been on her mind for more than a week. She could kick herself now.

So, the question was, would it be fair to tell Owen that she and the baby were now a package deal?

Abby could feel her heart crumbling.

What was she going to do? She lowered her face to her hands. Then a bright thought dragged her from the depths.

Jess. She needed to talk to Jess. Jess was sensible, logical. She wouldn't let emotion get in her way. She wouldn't let two weeks of pregnancy hormones cloud her thinking.

She'd call Jess.

Abby marched into the bedroom she and Owen now shared, and flopped across the bed on her stomach. Grabbing the phone off the far nightstand, she punched the phone number and waited for Jess's secretary to connect them.

"Jess Morgan."

Abby's voice caught in her throat at the sound of her friend's voice. "Jess?"

"Abby? That you? What's wrong? You sound awful. Don't tell me you have strep again."

Abby brushed away the hair that had fallen forward into her eyes. "No," she said, her voice steadier. "I don't have strep."

"But you're calling me for a definite reason?" Jess said suspiciously.

"Yeah." Abby swallowed. "Guess what."

Jess moaned. "Don't tell me, you're getting married."

Abby laughed, though there was nothing funny about her situation. "Well, I was. Now I don't know."

"Aw, Abby," Jess's voice softened. "Don't tell me it's

going badly already. I knew I should have gone to that house myself and picked those things up for you. I knew you shouldn't have gone back."

"No." Abby wiped at her eyes again. "No, Owen's been wonderful. He asked me to marry him again."

"But now you don't know if you want to?" Jess questioned. "Honey, it's only natural that you'd have second thoughts. Just because you love a man doesn't mean you can live with him. You'd be a fool not to think twice about remarrying the man you left."

Abby held her breath, waiting to get a word in. "Jess, I'm pregnant."

There was silence on the other end of the line.

"Did you hear me?" Abby asked.

"Crap."

Again, Abby laughed. She couldn't help herself.

"You're kidding! How can you be pregnant? You told me you were on the pill."

"I am. Guess it doesn't always work," she said sheepishly.

"But you've been there barely three weeks. How could you get yourself knocked up so fast?"

Abby rolled onto her back, bringing the phone to rest on her stomach. "I guess I hit it just right. I must have been ovulating the weekend I got here."

"Oh, boy, oh, boy," Jess muttered. "I take it Owen is not pleased."

"I haven't told him yet," she said in a small voice.

"You didn't tell him?"

Abby heard a banging on the phone as if Jess was hitting the receiver against her desk. "Hello? Anyone home?" Bang. Bang. "You didn't tell him?"

"Jess, he asked me to marry him, but he doesn't want children," she said with a lump in her throat. "I can't do this to him."

"Oh." This time Jess sounded deflated.

"I . . . I was thinking about going ahead to the beach house."

"Without telling him? Abby, that's a bad idea."

"Jess, he's been so happy. We've been so happy together. This will ruin everything. You know Owen, upstanding man that he is. He never even pays his electric bill late. He'll do the right thing. He'll marry me anyway."

"Whether he really wants to or not," Jess suggested quietly.

Tears sprang in Abby's eyes again. "Maybe it would just be better if I told him I changed my mind and left." She twisted the cord around her finger. She felt as if she were falling, turning, spinning, out of control. This wasn't supposed to happen. This wasn't part of the plan.

"Right now I know he loves me," Abby explained. "I know he wants to be with me. I could take that with me when I go. It would hurt, hurt us both, but it wouldn't hurt as much as being trapped in a marriage he didn't want. That would be worse for both of us. All three of us," she amended.

"I don't know about this, Abby," Jess hedged. "I suppose it makes sense if you try to look at it logically, but I don't know that it's the right thing to do." She paused. "You've discussed this, right? He's told you he doesn't want children?"

"I wanted children ten years ago, Jess. He kept telling me it wasn't the right time, but he was just putting me off. His mother and I just had a conversation last week. She thought that was one of the reasons we broke up the first time."

"I don't know." Jess's voice was thoughtful.

Abby's stomach twisted into knots. "All he's done since he took this softball team is talk about how he's not good with children."

"All right, all right. And I don't suppose you would consider any other options."

"Of course not! This is Owen's baby. Our baby. I'm going to have our baby."

"Being a single mother," Jess sounded close to tears now. "It's going to be hell."

"I can do it."

Abby could almost hear Jess smile sadly. "I know you can, honey."

A silence full of emotion hung between them.

"You want to come back here for a few days?" Jess finally asked. "You could stay with me. Just until you get your head screwed on straight." She gave a laugh, trying to lighten the conversation. "We could shop for baby strollers and crap like that."

"No, thanks. I think I'll drive on to the cottage. My book is going well. I don't want to lose my rhythm."

Jess sighed. "You sure this is what you want to do?"

Abby's lower lip trembled as she stared at the ceiling fan. "I'm sure."

"So, when are you going?"

"I don't know."

"Call me when you get there?"

"Sure. Thanks, Jess."

"Later, girlfriend."

Abby hung up the phone, but remained on the bed. She watched the fan spin round and round.

Now what should she do?

Work today? Have dinner with Owen as if nothing had happened? Make love with him tonight and then get up and leave in the morning?

No. She couldn't do that. She'd break down into tears. He'd convince her to tell him what was wrong.

She made herself get out of bed. She walked to the dresser she and Owen shared and opened the top drawer. Only yesterday she had put clothes in this drawer.

Dry-eyed with resolution, she began to pack.

"Abby?" Owen came in the front door, swinging his portfolio case. He'd had a great day and he couldn't wait to tell her about it.

Edgar met him in the front hall.

"Hey, how's my big boy?" Owen went down on one knee to scratch the Bernese behind the ears. "Where's Ab, huh, boy? Where's our Abby?"

Edgar looked up at him and chuffed softly.

Owen left his leather case inside the office door and went into the kitchen. The lights were out.

Her car hadn't been in the driveway, but he had assumed it was out back. He went into the mudroom to glance out the window. She wasn't parked in the back either.

"Hmmm," he said aloud.

He returned to the kitchen. That was strange. She had gone out, but not left a note. He told her he'd be home by six. It was only 5:45. Maybe she'd run to the grocery store or something. Maybe she hadn't left a note because she expected to be home before him. Oh well, he was sure she would be home shortly.

"Let's see, what can we make for dinner?" He went to the refrigerator and opened it up. "What shall we make, boy?"

Edgar thrust his nose into the fridge.

"What are your feelings about stuffed peppers? The Nesters gave us enough green peppers from their garden to feed a small foreign nation."

Humming to himself, Owen began to gather the ingredients he would need. He'd make dinner and surprise Abby when she got home—candlelight, soft music, the whole thing. He smiled to himself. A good day with work, a nice dinner, a little conversation on the front porch, and then a long evening in bed with Abby before sleep—life was good.

Life was damned near perfect.

At eight o'clock Owen blew out the candles on the dining room table. He left the covered casserole dish where it was in the center of the table, still filled with stuffed peppers, now gone cold. He pushed in his chair, scraping wood against wood and flipped off the light.

An hour ago he had wondered if he ought to call the police, maybe the hospital, just to be certain Abby hadn't been in an accident. But the longer he sat with the lettuce in the salad wilting, the sauce over the peppers congealing, the closer he came to the cold realization of what had happened.

Abby had left him. She was gone.

Again.

She said she still loved him. She said she had forgiven him for his past transgressions and that she wanted to marry him again.

It hadn't been true. Sentenced for a crime he didn't know he'd committed. Condemned without a trial. He slammed the back of the chair and it hit the table with a resounding thud.

Owen moved through the house, locking doors and shutting off lights. Edgar lumbered behind him, seeming to sense not just his master's anger, but his profound sadness as well.

Damn it! How could Abby do this?

He climbed the stairs and went into the bathroom. The moment he flipped on the light, he spotted the post-it note on the mirror. Why hadn't he thought to come upstairs? In the old days, she had always left him notes in the bathroom.

He hesitated in the doorway, not wanting to read the piece of paper. He could see from here that there were only a couple of words on it; he just couldn't make them out.

Owen felt sick to his stomach though he'd eaten nothing. His eyes were scratchy. He felt as if the bottom had dropped out of his world. What happened? She had seemed so happy. They'd both been happy.

He made himself cross the bathroom and yank the note off the mirror.

I changed my mind, it read simply. *So sorry. Abby*

Owen crumbled the note in his fist and threw it hard into the wastebasket.

He wiped at his eyes with the back of his hand.

That's it? She changed her mind? His sadness began to ebb, and in its place came renewed anger.

She'd changed her mind?

Changed her mind about what? Loving him? Did she mean she didn't love him? Or did she mean she didn't think the marriage could work? Either way, he deserved more of an explanation than one that could fit on a post-it note! Owen ground his teeth. Since the day Abby had left him the first time he had accepted the responsibility for the break-up of their marriage. He'd taken it all. But it hadn't all been his fault. If Abby had just come to him sooner, spoken louder, made him listen maybe . . .

But no, she'd just left without talking to him, without at least attempting to make him understand. And now she'd done it again.

He used the bathroom and went into the bedroom.

Maybe he just needed to get some sleep. He wasn't thinking clearly right now. He was so angry, so shocked, that he couldn't put two reasonable thoughts together. He'd never been one to act on anger and he couldn't now. Not with so much at stake.

He considered calling Ben or Zack, but he wasn't ready to tell anyone. Not yet.

He stared at the bed. Edgar slumped against him, coming to rest on his shoe. Dog and master stared at the neatly made bed.

Owen couldn't do it. He couldn't sleep there, not after making love with Abby there last night.

He shut out the light and went downstairs again. The only other bed in the house was the one from Abby's girlhood, and he certainly didn't want to sleep there. He went into the living room, clicked on the TV and stripped off his clothes. He lay on the couch in the darkness and pulled an afghan over him. He stared at the TV blankly.

It was going to be a long night.

Abby stumbled into Jess's family's cottage after midnight. She had intended to take two days to make the drive there, then decided to press on. Truthfully, she didn't trust herself. She was afraid that if she didn't put as much distance between her and Owen as possible, she'd turn her old Buick around and head straight back to Land's End.

Maybe that was what she should have done.

"God, you're such a coward," she murmured to herself as she moved sleepily through the house.

Following the instructions posted in the kitchen, Abby turned on the water pump at the circuit breaker box, brushed her teeth and fell into bed. She was so tired that she was certain she would fall asleep right away. But once she hit the pillow in the master bedroom, she couldn't close her eyes. She'd had a Coke an hour ago because she was feeling sleepy. Now the caffeine had kicked in.

She stared in the darkness at the ceiling in the unfamiliar room as tears welled in her eyes. She hadn't cried all day. Why now?

She thought of Owen and her heart wrenched in her chest. What had his reaction been when he arrived home to find her gone? The thought of his pain brought a fresh stream of tears tumbling down her cheeks.

Had she done the right thing?

It was too late now for second thoughts. It was done. Surely, she'd hurt Owen beyond reconciliation now.

Maybe it was better to think that way. If she believed she had no other choice at this point, maybe it would make going forward easier.

Then she thought about what Jess had said about how doing the logical thing wasn't always the right thing. She was right, wasn't she? Emotions weren't always logical. People weren't either.

It wasn't until that moment that Abby realized she'd done it again. Just like the first time, she'd walked out without a word. Without an explanation. Without even a good fight. She'd abandoned Owen and his love for her rather than face him.

At least a fight would have cleared the air, gotten everything out in the open.

She really was a coward. She'd been unfair to Owen as well as herself.

Abby rolled onto her side thinking of the tiny life inside her. "Oh, Owen," she sobbed into her pillow. "I'm so sorry."

Eighteen

After a night on the couch of bad movies, infomercials and nature channel segments on the reproduction cycle of flies, Owen finally fell asleep at dawn. He slept until mid-morning, waking with a jolt.

The afghan had fallen to the living room floor, and Edgar lay sleeping on it. Hearing his master stir, the dog woke and gazed up apologetically. He did not, however, return the blanket.

"Glad someone slept," Owen grumbled. He swung his bare legs over the edge of the couch and sat up, covering his face with his hands.

Edgar rose and chuffed. He needed to go outside.

Owen padded barefoot into the front hall, through the kitchen and into the mudroom. He opened the back door to let the dog out. His mother waved from the clothesline in her backyard.

Owen forced a "good son" smile, waved back and quickly closed the door. The last thing he needed this morning was a visit from his well-meaning, but throw-salt-in-the-wound mother. If she caught wind of Abby's departure, she'd be full of "I just knews" and other unproductive comments.

In the kitchen, Owen put the kettle on for tea, then decided on coffee. He was going to need a hard kick of caffeine this morning. As he waited for the pot to boil, he leaned against the counter.

Well, it was a new day and no prophetic revelations had come to him concerning Abby's hasty departure. And this morning he didn't know how he felt about it. Last night, somewhere between a fishing lure sales pitch and a wrestling match, his anger had once again ebbed. This morning he was just feeling hurt again. Hurt and a little lost.

He liked the anger better. When a person was angry he could curse, throw things, shout at the dog. This feeling was one of such helplessness.

He had to do something . . . but what? Last time he'd just let Abby go. His pride had prevented him from finding out why she left. He couldn't let that happen again.

He wondered what Abby wanted him to do. What was she expecting him to do? The way she left made him think she just wanted to cut things off between them. Obviously she didn't want to discuss the problem.

But what right did she have to make that decision for them? Didn't he deserve an explanation? He felt a flare of anger again.

The kettle whistled and he dug in a cupboard, unearthing a small jar of instant coffee. He measured a spoon into a mug and poured boiling water over it.

He still couldn't believe Abby would leave without word. Hadn't she learned anything from their last break-up? He sure as hell had.

Hadn't she felt the need to talk to anyone?

Then a thought occurred to him.

Jess.

That was who he ought to call. Jess was Abby's best friend. Abby was originally headed for Jess's house in Myrtle Beach. Surely, she would have told Jess if she were going after all.

Owen strode into his office, carrrying his cup of coffee. He didn't have Jess's number at work, but it was easy enough to call operator assistance. He knew what firm she worked for.

Within two minutes Jess picked up the phone. "Good morning, Jess Morgan."

"Jess, it's Owen . . . Owen Thomas."

There was a pause. "I know which Owen."

"Jess, I'm sorry to call you at work, but I've got to know what the hell is going on here. What happened?"

"What happened where? To whom?"

He took a chance. "Look, I know Abby called you. I know you know what's going on here." He tried not to sound as if he were angry with Jess. "At least, you have better clue than I do."

She exhaled. "You need to talk to Abby, not me."

"So, she did go to Myrtle Beach?"

"Yeah," she answered reluctantly. "She called me from here this morning to let me know she'd made it safely."

"There's a phone there?" he asked, feeling a trickle of hope. "I could call her?"

"Sorry. No phone. It's not been reconnected."

"So, how the hell did she call you?" he snapped.

There was silence on the other end.

"I'm sorry," Owen apologized. "That was uncalled

for." He traced his and Abby's names on his blotter with his finger and had to force down the lump that rose in his throat. It was coming again, that feeling of discouragement. "It's just that I'm going crazy. I thought things were good between us again. I thought they were great. She said she wanted to get married again. Then I come home and she's gone. No warning. Nothing. She shouldn't have left without an explanation, Jess. She should have talked to me," he said firmly.

Jess was quiet.

He tried to stay calm despite the pounding of his heart and took a different tack. "Jess, did something happen? Something I don't know about?" If one of the guys said something to Abby, he'd kill them. "Come on, Jess, help me out here. I love her, I love her more than anything on God's green earth."

"You do, don't you?" Jess said softly, a certain wistfulness in her voice.

"More than the ocean loves the sand." And he meant it. Despite his anger, he still loved her desperately.

"God, that's sweet." Jess took a breath. "No matter what the circumstances?" she questioned. "Even if things aren't the way you think they are?"

He pulled on the phone cord. "I have no idea what you're talking about, but nothing could change how I feel about her. Nothing could make me not want to live with her for the rest of my life." Thoughts began to pop into his head. Frightening thoughts. "Oh, hell, Jess. Don't tell me she's sick. Really sick?"

Jess chuckled. "It's one of those illnesses that will pass."

His patience was beginning to slip. "Are you going to tell me what's going on or am I going to have to—"

"What?" she challenged. "What are you going to do?"

"I don't know!" he burst out. "It's an empty threat. You know it. I know it." He softened his tone. "Please, Jess, just tell me what's wrong. Why did Abby leave me again?"

He heard her switch him to the speakerphone, then the sound of her lighting up a cigarette. "You sitting down?" she asked.

Every muscle in his body tightened as he sat up straight in the chair. "Let me have it."

It was only 9:30 when Owen hung up the phone. If he hurried and didn't break too many speed limits and get arrested, he could make it to Myrtle Beach by this evening. He grabbed the portable phone and dialed Zack as he went upstairs to change and throw clothes into a bag.

"Buddy," he said when Zack answered the phone.

"Hey, what's up?"

"I need you to take Edgar for a day or two, maybe longer. Can you handle it?"

"You going somewhere?" Zack kept his tone casual, but Owen knew he knew something was wrong.

Owen walked into the bathroom to gather a couple of toiletries. "She's gone, Zack. Abby left me again."

"I'll be right there."

Owen heard the click as Zack disconnected. He'd have just enough time to shower and dress before his buddy arrived.

Sure enough, just as Owen came down the stairs still towel-drying his hair, Zack walked in the front door.

"What happened, buddy?"

"Come on upstairs, I'll fill you in while I finish packing."

While stuffing clothing into his duffel bag, Owen gave Zack a rundown of what happened. As he zipped his bag closed, he turned to his friend. "Now, if you're going to start in on me about how I'd be better off without her and just pay child-support, I don't want to hear it."

Zack frowned. "Actually, what I was going to say is that you need to get your butt to Myrtle Beach. You guys love each other too much to let misunderstandings and miscommunications get in the way of that kind of love."

"This coming from a confirmed bachelor?" They went down the stairs and into the front hall.

"Hey, we're all different." He touched Owen's shoulder. "You love her. This is what makes you happy." He nodded. "You owe it to yourself to try to make it work. The one thing I can tell you is that being a father . . ." He paused. "It's the best."

Owen smiled. "Thanks."

"Hey, the dog's no problem."

Owen met his friend's gaze. "You know what I mean." Then he was out the door.

Abby sat down and dug her feet in the sand. The sun had set behind her. Only the lights from the cottages in the dunes lighted the shore. The tide was coming in, easing further up the beach with each incoming wave.

It had been a beautiful day for sunbathing, reading a

the beach or working on her laptop on the porch over-looking the ocean. But she'd gotten nothing done. She'd not been able to enjoy the crash of the waves, the smell of the salt spray or the call of the seagulls. All day she had felt immobilized, unable to do anything, unable to even think.

She had opened her laptop at noon, but hadn't typed a word. She had tried to get back into a book she'd started reading in Land's End, but it hadn't held her attention. It was a wasted day. She'd not even unpacked her car. Mostly, she'd just sat in the sand and stared out at the ocean.

She was miserable. She was scared and she wanted Owen. She knew she could be a mother, even a good one, but the thought was still daunting. She should never have left Land's End without telling him about the baby. Hadn't she learned anything from the last time? Now, sitting here in the sand, forcing herself to look at her own behavior she realized that she'd placed most, if not all, of the blame for their divorce on Owen. It had been so easy to do; he'd been so willing to accept it. But the truth was, the divorce was Abby's fault, too. It was her fault because she'd not made him listen to her. In the end, she'd not even spoken up. Everything she'd ever read about marriages talked about men not being good com-municators, but women could have the same fault, too, couldn't they?

Abby stared out into the darkness at the crashing waves. "Oh, Owen," she whispered. "What have I done?"

What had she done? She knew exactly what she'd done. The question was, what would she do now? It was time to stop being a coward.

So, did she call him? Did she get back in the car and drive to Maryland? Would he even see her when she got there after what she'd done to him?

Abby rose to her feet, gazing at the white foam of the outgoing wave that had just crashed on the beach. No, a phone call wasn't right. This was a conversation that needed to be conducted face-to-face. She turned on her heels with determination and started up the dune toward the cottage.

Halfway to the house, Abby saw a man coming down the porch steps, walking straight toward her.

It couldn't be . . .

Owen was in Land's End.

"Abby!" The silhouette of the man called to her.

Her voice caught in her throat. "Owen?"

It *was* Owen!

She raced across the sand in the darkness. He came toward her. She had seen movies where this happened all the time, but never once had those old movies come close to describing how she felt at this moment.

Owen swept her into his arms. Tears ran down her cheeks and she rested her head on his shoulder. He felt so good, so strong and sturdy. No matter what happened, no matter what he wanted to do, she knew everything was going to be all right.

"I'm so sorry. I did it to you again." The words came spilling out of her.

He grasped her arms, drawing back so that he could look her in the eye. "Why didn't you tell me about the baby?" he demanded.

"You know?" She stared at him, trying to make out his expression by the dim light of the porch.

"Don't blame Jess." He let go of her.

She could tell he was angry.

"She didn't want to tell me," he said.

"I can't believe you came all the way here." Abby looked down at her bare feet in the sand.

"Of course I came all this way. I came all this way because I deserve an explanation from the woman I love."

Now she could see into his blue eyes. They were filled with a tumult of emotion and not just anger. She saw relief, sadness, fear, joy and love. All the things she was feeling at this very moment.

So there was hope.

"Why didn't you tell me?" he demanded. "Why did you just take off like this?"

Tears filled her eyes and she wiped at them. "Because I know you don't want children. I didn't want to ruin everything."

He gestured harshly. "Who said I didn't want children?"

She pushed the hair out of her face, realizing that she had made a bigger mistake than she thought. "Well, when we were married before, I kept asking about children. You kept brushing me off, saying 'someday.' "

"I was just too damned wrapped up in my career. I never meant we weren't going to have children. I just assumed that would be later in the future."

"But your mother said—"

"My mother? I've never had a discussion in my life with my mother about being a father. And even if I had, why would you take her word on anything so important as this?"

Abby shook her head, trying to explain, realizing there

was no good explanation. "And then with the softball team, you kept saying you weren't good with kids. When Tonesha got hurt you said you could never be a parent."

"Abby!" He grasped her shoulders and made her look at him "I made that comment in passing. I didn't mean I didn't want children. I just meant that I thought it must be hard to be in the position Tonesha's parents were in."

She tried to process what he was saying, coming to the full realization of what a huge mistake she'd made. "You mean you do want children?"

"Of course I want children! *Your children.*"

"I can't believe I did this." She dropped her face into her hands, a fresh flood of tears welling up again. "You're right. I know you're right. I was so scared; I just didn't know how to tell you. I was so afraid that if you didn't want the baby—"

"Aw, sweetheart, don't cry." He pushed her hands away and wiped at her tears with his fingers, drawing her into his arms. "There's no harm done that we can't fix together."

"I just can't believe I did this." She looked up into his gentle blue eyes. "I guess you're not the only one that needed to change to make this work."

He groaned and pulled her tightly against his chest. "Abby, please don't feel that there's anything you can't tell me or ask me." He took one of her hands in his and kissed her knuckles. Her tears were making his tee shirt wet. "You've got to tell me what's going on in that head of yours. You tell me what you're thinking, what you feel, and I'll tell you. It's the only way this marriage can work."

She threw her arms around his neck to hug him. He

was right; every word he said was right. She had been wrong, so wrong. "You're a good man, Owen Thomas."

He stroked her back and they met nose-to-nose. "I guess this means the wedding needs to be sooner rather than later," he teased, lowering his hand to her flat abdomen.

She laughed through her tears that were now tears of joy. "I love you, Owen."

"I love you, Ab," he said fiercely.

Then he took her mouth with his. It was the sweetest kiss, one full of past memories and better yet, the promise of a future.

Please turn the page for
an exciting sneak peek at the
second installment of Bachelors, Inc.
TEMPTING ZACK
coming from Bouquet
in October 2000

One

"Want to give me a hand?" Zack Taylor called to his daughter as he carried some gardening tools from his shed.

Pigtailed, ten-year-old Savannah sat on the back step of their Victorian house, petting Piper, one of her cats. She wrinkled her nose. "Do I have to?"

"No, you don't have to," he said casually. "It's just that I could use some help." If there was one thing Zack had learned after all these years of being a single parent, it was that children like to feel they have some control over their lives, even if it is just with the little things.

She rose from the step. "What are you planting?"

"I'm working on an English herb garden." He continued carrying hand tools from the gardening shed. "I'll start the plants inside the greenhouse and transplant them in the spring."

Next to Savannah, Zack's garden was his pride and joy. His parents had bought the empty lot behind them when he was a child. Thanks to their forethought, the already large lot on a shady street in the Chesapeake town of Land's End was double the size of the others. His parents had given him the home when they'd moved to California to retire. It had provided plenty of open space for Savannah to play in during their weekend visits from Annapolis. Now that they lived here permanently, Zack was able to expand his overgrown garden into the empty back lot.

"What are you planting?" Savannah asked again as she plopped down on a stone bench where he'd left his flat of seedlings.

"Let's see." He glanced at the flat. "Foxglove, parsley, sage"—he began to sing—"rosemary and thyme."

She wrinkled her freckled nose. "Simon and Garfunkle freak."

"Stone Cold Tossing Pumpkins freak," he shot back.

She rolled her eyes dramatically. "Dad, it's not 'Stone Cold Tossing Pumpkins.' They're the Cold Stones. You know that."

"Sorry. It's just that when I was a kid, bands had simpler names."

She laughed. "What are you talking about? You listen to Grandpa's music. I'm surprised we don't listen to Laurence Welk when we have dinner."

"Your grandfather never liked Laurence Welk, I can assure you. He was an Elvis fan all the way."

Zack stepped into the greenhouse he'd built with his own hands. It had been designed by one of his best friends, Owen, an architect, and was reminiscent of an old Victorian greenhouse from the turn of the century. "Want to bring that flat in?"

Savannah carried the seedlings into the greenhouse, dropped them on a wooden workbench and wandered out again. The sliding windows were open on two sides so Zack could talk to her as he worked. This was his favorite way to spend Sunday afternoons, his hands in the soil, his daughter nearby.

"So, how's school going?" he asked.

"Too easy."

Through the window he could see that she had hopped up on the stone bench and was walking back and forth across it, arms outstretched like a tightrope walker.

"Well, you're only two weeks into the new school year. You know how it is, teachers need to figure out where students are. There's a lot of reviewing."

"I thought that was why I was in a family group." She pivoted and walked across the bench again. "This is my second year with Mrs. Farley. She knows I read on a ninth-grade level."

Zack dumped some potting soil into a bucket and added a cup of organic manure. Savannah participated in a program in her elementary school where students remained in the same classroom for three years at a time with the same teacher. The program was set up to offer more consistency in the education system and more time on task. So far, Zack was very pleased; it was working out much better than the typical classroom system she'd been in when they lived in Annapolis.

"I know you're not bragging because my daughter wouldn't do that."

"Not bragging, just stating the facts, Dad."

Zack heard a sound on the roof and glanced out the open window. She had disappeared from sight. Savannah had apparently used the bench as a stepping stone to climb onto the roof of the greenhouse. He glanced up to see her silhouetted through the reinforced glass panes, his fatherly defense mechanism immediately going up. She knew better.

"What are you doing up there? Get down," he called. "You're going to fall and break your legs."

"I'm not going to fall."

Zack continued to mix the soil and manure with a special aerating tool and used his best "daddy" voice. "Savannah Jane!"

He heard her groan the way she did when she thought he was being utterly ridiculous. "All right! I'll—"

Zack heard her fall and looked up in time to see her slip down the pitched roof. "Savannah!" he hollered, dropping the tool. He ran for the door.

Savannah hit the ground before he could get to her, landing between the bench and the greenhouse.

"Savannah! You all right?" He went down on his knees in the grass, gathering her in his arms. She was crying.

"I'm sorry, Dad," she managed through tears. "I should have listened to you."

"All right, all right." His heart was pounding in his chest, but he knew he needed to stay calm. As long as he stayed calm, Savannah wouldn't get too upset. "Just sit still and let me see how many legs you broke."

Tears ran down her cheeks. "My legs aren't broken see." She moved both legs. "But my arm really hurts. I think I hit it on the bench."

"Hold still." Cradling her in his arms as he had when she was an infant, he carefully lifted her forearm to examine it. It was already swelling between her wrist and elbow.

"Bummer, dude," he said, still keeping it light. Hi

guess was that it was broken. "Looks like a Sunday afternoon x-ray trip to me."

"No, Dad, it'll be all right." She stood up, her cheeks still wet with tears. "I'm sorry. That was so stupid to do."

"Just the same, you need an x-ray, sweetie." He ushered her toward his restored Volkswagen microbus parked out back.

"Do I have to?" Savannah whimpered, wiping at her tears.

"You have to." She'd just scared him half to death, but his heart had finally slowed to a normal pace. If all she had gotten out of this misadventure was a broken arm, he knew they were lucky.

He opened the passenger door and helped her jump in, taking care with her injured arm. "Humor me on this call and after we're done in the ER, we'll go for a frozen yogurt." He closed her door. "Deal, Baby Bear?" he asked through her open window.

It was their secret endearment they used only in private.

She gave him half a smile. She was looking so much older these days, but at this moment she just looked like a scared little girl. "Deal, Daddy Bear."

"I understand that, ma'am," Zack said tersely to the ER receptionist. "But it's been more than an hour since the x-ray was taken. I want to know if her arm is broken or not." He pressed his palms on the counter. "I don't understand why this is taking so long."

The woman gazed over the rims of her wire-frame glasses and blinked as if he were speaking Apache. She apparently was unfamiliar with the linguistics of this Native American tribe.

"How much longer?" he asked when she didn't respond. "If it is broken, I'd like to see it set before the bones begin knitting together again."

Another blink.

He was normally a calm, laid-back kind of guy, but this waiting was making him crazy. Savannah could have a serious break and he still didn't know anything. He needed a nice cup of chamomile tea to settle his nerves and get himself centered again. He took a deep breath. "Could you at least check for me?" He motioned to the busy room behind her.

From where he stood, he could see nurses walking back and forth, pushing carts and carrying supplies. An orderly pushed a man in a wheelchair past him. The ER appeared to be open and running; there was just no progress on Zack's end.

The receptionist smoothed the tight bun in her hair and rose from her seat. She slowly walked from view in her sensible shoes.

Zack tapped his fingers on the countertop, then saw how dirty they were and lowered them to his sides. They had gotten dirty from the potting soil he'd been mixing. He needed to go to the restroom and wash them, but he didn't want to leave Savannah alone in the waiting room. What if they called her name?

The receptionist shuffled back to the desk. She sat down and took her time straightening two pens on her blotter before peering over her glasses at him again. "Dr. Kayla Burns will see your daughter next. She asked that you please have a seat and someone will call you in approximately five minutes."

Zack felt another flicker of irritation. "Kayla Burns? A woman?"

Blink. "She appears to be, sir."

He frowned. "You haven't got any male doctors back here?"

Her monotone voice never changed. There was not a hint of inflection in her speech. She could have been a robot for all Zack knew. "Dr. Burns is the ER physician on call today, sir."

"There's no men on staff here?" he asked in disbelief.

"Midnight. We work twelve hour shifts here, sir." Blink. "You want to wait?"

He exhaled. "No, of course not. Fine." He slapped his hand on the counter. "I'll let my little girl know someone is finally going to examine her."

Dr. Kayla Burns glanced up from the chart she was completing. She had to use the bathroom, but she wanted to get this case taken care of before she took the break she had needed an hour ago. "Yes, Rosy?"

"Just a warning, Doc. You've got a woman-hater coming your way."

Kayla chuckled. She loved Rosy. The woman dressed, spoke, moved like an android, but she ran the ER with a proficiency that couldn't be bought for love or money.

"That right? The drunk with the head laceration?"

Rosy glanced over the rims of her glasses as she always did and Kayla wondered if they served any purpose but to accentuate her long nose. The woman never actually looked through the lenses. "No. The kid with the broken arm. The father."

Kayla lifted her brow. "The one with the tie-dyed T-shirt and the cute ponytail?"

Rosy lifted her hand, making a familiar sign with two fingers. "Peace, man." She never even cracked a smile.

Kayla cackled with laughter. It really wasn't that funny but a single woman pushing forty without any husband prospects in sight had to take her laughs where she could find them. "Will you find me the x-ray and let me have a look-see?" She tapped the chart on the counter in front of her. "I'll be done with this in a sec and then I have to run to the ladies room."

"Anything else, Dr. Burns?"

"Sure, Rosy. A date for the Auxiliary dinner/dance next Saturday night."

Rosy blinked. "Can't help you there, Doc. I don't look good in a tux."

Kayla was still chuckling to herself when she went into the unisex bathroom off the ER. The hospital had been built only two years ago and the administration had been very hip in their vision. The staff hated the unisex bathrooms, but Kayla kind of liked them. She always met the most interesting people in the bathrooms.

"I'll be right back, OK?" Zack asked Savannah.

She didn't even look up from the book she'd brought in with her. She shifted the ice pack on her arm. "Whatever."

Surprised to find no door that was labeled "Ladies" or

"Gentlemen," he pushed into the door simply labeled "Restroom."

At the sink he squirted soap on his hands and began to rub them vigorously. A toilet flushed in the row of stalls behind him and he heard a door swing open.

An attractive dark-haired woman walked up to the basin beside him and reached for the soap. "Excuse me," she said.

Zack glanced in the mirror at her. She was a pretty woman—his age, maybe a little older—and wore her hair pulled back in a ponytail. Her face was heart-shaped with dark eyes that had a certain sparkle in them. It was almost as if she knew a little secret she wouldn't share with the world. It was her eyes that held his attention even more than the hemp fabric T-shirt that clung to her breasts.

It wasn't often that Zack took much notice of women. Since his divorce he'd pretty much stayed clear of them. After his best friends Owen and Ben joined him in forming a business that restored old homes, he'd sworn off of them for good. He and his friends had even made this kind of pact not to date. They called their company Bachelors, Incorporated. Of course Owen had already fallen from grace. Just last month he had remarried his ex-wife and they were now living in newlywed bliss.

There was something about this woman that prevented him from looking away. Had he really been without a partner so long that he was eyeing women in public bathrooms?

It was a pathetic little life, but it was his.

The woman dried her hands and walked to a door on the opposite side of the bathroom labeled "Staff only."

He watched her hips sway in blue jeans that hugged her curves just right.

Nice. Very nice.

Zack was just walking back into the waiting room when someone called Savannah's name. "Ready, sweetie?"

Savannah slid her bookmark between the pages and got up. "Ready, Dad."

They followed a nurse into a brightly painted examining room and Savannah hopped up on the exam table.

"Dr. Burns will be right with you," the nurse said and backed out of the room with a smile.

In less than five minutes the door swung open. "Good afternoon, sorry for the wait," the doctor said, entering the room.

Zack glanced up, then took a double take. Dr. Burns was the woman in the bathroom.

ABOUT THE AUTHOR

Colleen Faulkner lives with her family in Delaware and is the author of twenty Zebra historical romances. She is currently working on TEMPTING ZACK and TAMING BEN, the next two installments of her Bachelors, Inc. trilogy. Colleen loves hearing from readers and you may write to her c/o Zebra Books. Please include a self-addressed stamped envelope if you wish a reply.

BOOK YOUR PLACE ON OUR WEBSITE AND MAKE THE READING CONNECTION!

We've created a customized website just for our very special readers, where you can get the inside scoop on everything that's going on with Zebra, Pinnacle and Kensington books.

When you come online, you'll have the exciting opportunity to:

- View covers of upcoming books

- Read sample chapters

- Learn about our future publishing schedule (listed by publication month *and author*)

- Find out when your favorite authors will be visiting a city near you

- Search for and order backlist books from our online catalog

- Check out author bios and background information

- Send e-mail to your favorite authors

- Meet the Kensington staff online

- Join us in weekly chats with authors, readers and other guests

- Get writing guidelines

- AND MUCH MORE!

**Visit our website at
http://www.zebrabooks.com**

Put a Little Romance in Your Life With
Fern Michaels

__Dear Emily	0-8217-5676-1	$6.99US/$8.50CAN
__Sara's Song	0-8217-5856-X	$6.99US/$8.50CAN
__Wish List	0-8217-5228-6	$6.99US/$7.99CAN
__Vegas Rich	0-8217-5594-3	$6.99US/$8.50CAN
__Vegas Heat	0-8217-5758-X	$6.99US/$8.50CAN
__Vegas Sunrise	1-55817-5983-3	$6.99US/$8.50CAN
__Whitefire	0-8217-5638-9	$6.99US/$8.50CAN

Put a Little Romance in Your Life With

Hannah Howell

__**Highland Destiny** 0-8217-5921-3	$5.99US/$7.50CAN
__**Highland Honor** 0-8217-6095-5	$5.99US/$7.50CAN
__**Highland Promise** 0-8217-6254-0	$5.99US/$7.50CAN
__**My Valiant Knight** 0-8217-5186-7	$5.50US/$7.00CAN
—**A Taste of Fire** 0-8217-5804-7	$5.99US/$7.50CAN
__**Wild Roses** 0-8217-5677-X	$5.99US/$7.50CAN